YOURS TO PROTECT

A PURE DECADENCE NOVEL

KELLY COLLINS

BOOK NOOK PRESS

PROLOGUE

The cigarette burns to my knuckles, but I don't flinch. The stench of burning skin fills the air before a flick of my wrist sends the hot ember into the street. I pull out a handful of pistachio nuts from my frayed front pocket and discard the shells onto the sidewalk. I train my eyes on the bungalow—waiting—watching. Where in the hell is she? I followed her to the party but lost her when she entered the building. "Invitation only," they said as I walked to the door. She disappeared into the crowd wearing a dress only a prostitute would wear. Stupid whore. It's four in the morning, and she's not tucked into her bed alone. She'll pay for this.

I wait for her all night to emerge from the building. I am always waiting for her. Countless times I put myself in her path, waiting for her to notice me, acknowledge me, but she always looks through me— past me—around me. *He* said she needed discipline. It may be the only thing *he* got right. I know her type —I raised one myself. A slow smile spreads across my face as I think about the ways I'll punish her. I can almost feel her hair wrapped around my hand as I drag her screaming, begging for mercy into my special place—a place I reserved for her alone. Just thinking about her tied up and defenseless gives me joy. I can imagine her screams for help. There will be no overlooking me then.

I lean against the tree and blend into the bark. My dark, hooded sweatshirt is the perfect camouflage as the car approaches. I watch for her, but as it passes, my rage surfaces. She's no different from my Rachel, who paid for her disobedience, and so would Roxanne. With a clenched fist, I slam my hand into the car window near me. The alarm wails, and I disappear as night becomes day.

CHAPTER ONE

Wrapped in Bobby's warm embrace, I refuse to move. Right here is where I want to be, pretending we're a couple. In my mind, we've been together for years, and in his arms is how I wake up every morning. We're inseparable. Even in sleep, he hangs on tightly. His grip on me is one of unbreakable possession. In my fantasy, he never lets me go.

Cocooned in his tattered black T-shirt, I curl into the warmth of his body in the center of the big bed. The morning light breaks through the curtains and shines like a spotlight on the royal-blue dress.

Last night's party was epic. The borrowed dress barely covered my body, but despite the lack of fabric, Bobby's eyes never left my face. He looked at me the way he did when we were teenagers. He saw me as no one else could.

"What are you so deep in thought about?" The rasp of his sleepy voice breaks the silence in the room.

My head settles into the cradle of his arm, and I swear the spot was custom made for me.

"I was thinking about the prom do-over last night. I had so much fun. You and I danced all night. I should say, we danced every minute we weren't kissing, but even then, the lines were blurred." The prom had come and gone without me. A sigh spills from my lips. He would've been the perfect date. "Did you go to our senior prom?"

"Yes, I went with Greta Salinger. She drank too much punch and ended up puking in my car." His nose scrunches at the word puke. "The band sucked. It was an early night. Last night was far more fun. Why didn't you go to our prom?"

"No one invited me." My father wouldn't have let me attend, anyway. "If anyone had asked, I would've had to say no. You of all people know how hard it is to get vetted by my family." I smile, but my heart isn't in it. The smile stops at my lips, never lifting to my eyes. In retrospect, I missed out on many things, prom notwithstanding. "The invite would've had to come my freshman year for the senior prom.

Even then, permission to attend would've been questionable."

"What's the deal with your dad?" Propping pillows behind us, he sits us against the headboard. I notice he keeps me close to his side. Sweet man. My fingertips trace his chest. The ripples of his muscles are like steel. "Is he still controlling?"

"I'm estranged from my family. No one talks to me." I pick at the hem of the T-shirt. Just like the cloth I'm wearing, I feel frayed and worn around the edges. Life is better this way. I get to live in blissful ignorance, and they don't have to deal with me anymore. I suppose it's a win for everyone. "I haven't seen them in years." It's funny how being alone can be blissful, but I'm better off alone given my upbringing with my obsessive father. It's better for everyone. It's safer for everyone.

"Wow, that had to be a lifestyle change. Is that why you bartend at Trax?" He shifts my body to look into his eyes. I could drown in the emerald-green pools. In high school, it had always been his eyes that held my attention. They were a beautiful color and in this morning's light, I can see that nothing's changed.

"Have you been checking up on me, Detective?" I never told him about bartending at Trax. He must have done some digging around. "I went from a princess to a pauper in the time it takes to exhale." I shimmy in closer to him, drawing the heat from his body to warm the iciness in my heart. Talk of my past always leaves me feeling cold. "It was a tough transition, but I'd do it again. I can make it rain cash because I work hard. I earn everything I have. The exception is that blue dress," I point to the slinky blue fabric hanging haphazardly across the chair, "that belongs to Emma."

"I owe Emma an enormous debt of gratitude." He releases a soft catcall between puckered lips. "When I saw you in that dress, I couldn't breathe. It's... it's—"

"Pornographic?"

His head nods in agreement. "Well, there is that, but I would say, not every girl could wear that dress well. You possess perfect breasts and a flawless body." His eyes take me in from head to toe. His gaze has the same effect as his lips skimming my skin—goose bumps. "The way the fabric clings to every curve of your body leaves no room for imagination. I couldn't take my eyes off you. You were perfection. You *are* perfection." His eyes close in a half-hooded way that screams sex. His lower lip slips between his teeth just as a soft groan escapes his mouth. His stare rakes over my body. "You look hot in that shirt, by the way. I'm sure you'd look hot in anything—hotter in nothing."

Sleeping in his T-shirt should reduce the sexy factor, but when he looks at me with such fierce passion, I feel hot—steaming hot. Who says a cotton shirt can't scream sexpot?

"It surprised me that you focused on my face. Every other man in the club never looked above my chest." I wrap my arms around him, pressing my chest into his side. I hear his breath hitch and smile. I would climb inside him if I could, but I settle for laying my head against him. The hairs of his chest against my cheek are enticing. His scent fills my nose and makes me feel like Aphrodite to his Ares.

He unwraps one of my arms from around his middle and slides his fingers through mine. He lifts my hand to his lips and kisses my knuckles. The sweet gesture pinches my heart. I never thought it possible to go back and relive the best thing from my past.

"When I was sixteen, I had the biggest crush on you. All I could think about was pressing my face into your breasts. Even back then, they were perfect. Now I'm an adult, and I know if I win your heart, I can have your breasts forever."

My laugh bubbles up from deep inside. "Listen to you. Your endgame is still the same. It's all about my boobs." I sit up and cross my arms over my chest. "You had me in your bed all night. Not once did you try to cop a feel. Why?" I would've done anything he wanted last night. I always had a thing for him. Every girl has a boy she dreams about, and Bobby was my wet dream.

With little effort, he pulls me into his lap and grips me like I belong to him, and he'll never let me go. "I never got over my crush, Roxanne. When Emma tracked me down at the precinct, it catapulted me back in time. I've thought of you hundreds of times. I fantasized about you walking back into my life, but I never thought it would happen. I don't want to be the sixteen-year old boy who loses the girl of his dreams again. You're more than an impressive set of tits." His eyes lower, and his voice softens. "Rumors ran rampant in high school about the Somerville sisters. I never completely understood why you couldn't see me. Help me understand."

Straddling his body, I cover his mouth with my lips. How can I explain something I don't understand myself? "Life as a Somerville has never been easy or without unique challenges." It's a weak answer. I wish I could elaborate, but I never understood my father's obsession to have absolute control over his women.

His lips find mine, and he gives me the kiss I've wanted for years. It's more than lips touching and tongues tangling. My future lies in its depth. How will I ever let him go? He pulls away, leaving me wanting more. Sitting on his lap, I can tell he wants more, too. If only he would take what I'm offering.

"Life is complicated, no matter who you are. The

universe throws things in our direction all the time. It's how we handle the hits that determine the outcome." I run my hands up his chest with pecs like cinderblocks; he's perfectly prepped for the hits.

His statement strikes a nerve. What's been my strategy for dealing with the "hits," as he calls them? Have I ever had a strategy outside of defiance and avoidance?

"What's been your biggest challenge since you graduated?" What does "hits" mean to him? Are they a short payday, or has he faced some real challenges? Has he ever been homeless or hungry? I have, and the experience is not worthy of a do-over.

"My biggest hit was when my mom was ill. She had to take unpaid leave from work. Dad was already gone, so my brothers and me had to step up and help. Juggling work and school was tough for all of us."

So, it was a short payday mixed with the stress of an ill parent and a job. Many mature men would struggle under that type of stress. "Is your mom okay?"

"My mom is fine. It was breast cancer, but things have been good since her surgery. She's been in remission for years."

"Wow, that must be a relief. How long was she ill?" My father's way of taking care of my mother is sending her off to treatment centers. Trenton Somerville is like cancer. Maybe if my mother had simply excised him from her life, she could be cured.

"Things were up and down for about a year. Mom having to endure the suffering was the worst part of the ordeal for me." A sorrowful look crosses his face. "I grew up a lot that year. It helped mold me into the man I am today. It was bad and good at the same time."

I brush my lips across his. If I could've taken away his pain, I would have. "Where did you work that you could support a family at such a young age?"

His eyes lift to the ceiling as if the answer might be there. "I worked for a private detective agency while I went to school. Ten dollars an hour doesn't finance much, so I lived at home, and we all pooled our resources. The twins worked, too. You do what you have to do to survive."

What an understatement. "Yep, I get it. Why a detective agency?" I can't imagine him staking out a house or tailing somebody. He's so noticeable. Nothing about Bobby blends into the background.

A light twinkles in his eye. "I was chomping at the bit to join the police force. They wouldn't hire me until I was twenty-one. It was as close as I could get to the real thing until I could get to the real thing." His tongue darts out to wet his lip. Damn, if I didn't wish I was his lip.

"What about you? Where did you go to school?"

Lost in the thought of his tongue, I struggle to answer.

"Earth to Roxanne? Are you with me?" His tone is playful. He plucks at my lower lip with his finger, drawing my attention back to the conversation.

"Hmm... yes... sorry... school." Getting my thoughts back on track, I skim over my college history. "I initially went to USC, and as expected, I entered law. Then everything kind of changed. I dropped out and made my way. I've been bartending for several years now." I'm surprised I gave him that much of an answer. I've learned over time, the less I say, the safer it is for everyone.

"There's a mystery there. One you don't seem ready to talk about, but I hope you'll trust me enough to tell me sometime soon. Right now, I have a nearly naked girl in my bed. The way her hand is rubbing my chest is driving me insane." He rolls us over and straddles my body, causing me to laugh. I haven't felt this lighthearted and free in years.

A charge crackles through the air. I look into his eyes, and it's as if our conversation never stopped. There are words in his eyes. My T-shirt bunches up around my waist, leaving my tummy exposed. The thin lace of my underwear is all that conceals my lower half.

His arousal strains against his sweatpants. The thought of making love to him sucks the air from my lungs. Will he be a good lover? Thinking of him with other women creates a powerful surge of jealousy. It's like bitch-eating sharks are swimming inside me, and I can't shake the feeling. I know I can't have him because I can't put him at risk. The consequences could be devastating.

I may not keep him, but I can have a few more kisses. What harm can a kiss bring?

My hands reach up to his bare chest, and my fingers dance over every muscle. His finely toned body comes from years of hard work and healthy eating.

Working at a gay bar, I hear lots of things about physique. He wouldn't last a second in Trax. Men would be all over him the minute he walked in the door. A three-inch smile spreads over my face. A laugh escapes my lips.

"What's so funny?" He pulls my hands from his chest and pushes them above my head. I'm pinned down, and the sensation of letting someone else have control is frightening and exciting at the same time.

"If you walked into Trax, the men would go mad over your sexy gutters." His eyes grow wide at my statement.

"What the hell is a sexy gutter?" He cocks his head to the side and waits for an answer.

I pull my hands free and run my fingertips over the indentations left by his well-defined musculature. I follow the line down to the finely cut V dipping below his waistband. "Sexy gutters are these grooves left behind when your muscles stand erect."

I choose my words carefully, and they dramatically influence him. Tiny bumps rise on the surface of his skin. The longer my hands stroke his body, the larger the bumps become. I feel his hardness jump in reaction to my words. I should make some excuse to leave and be on my way, but I can't help myself. I feel like a magnet, and he's solid steel.

"Hmm, I've never heard them called cum gutters, but then again, I don't hang out in gay bars."

"You don't know what you're missing. Some of my best friends are gay men." My thumbs graze across his nipples, making him shiver. He pulls my hands and pins them above my head again.

"I know lots of gay men. I call several of them friends. I don't partake in the same pleasures. I love women." He drops his head and lowers his lips to my neck. Bumps rise on my skin now. His warm tongue traces my collarbone to my shoulder and back. His lips travel up my neck to the triple pierced lobe of my ear. The tingly sensation crawls down my spine until it plants itself in the throbbing apex of my thighs.

How long has it been since I've given myself to a man? It's been at least a year. If I close my eyes, I can see his face. His hair was dark and his body stocky, but his name remains a mystery. Anonymity has always been prudent.

His lips trace my jawline and come to rest on my chin. Did I close my eyes? They flutter open in time to watch him close his. As soon as his lips meet mine, all thoughts of gay men and past lovers are gone. This man is not into other men. Right now, he's into me, and I don't have the willpower to stop him. Doesn't every girl deserve a selfish moment?

CHAPTER TWO

Bobby peppers me with kisses until I want to explode. Things move like he invented time. He works at his pace, for his purpose, and my pleasure. With my hands pinned above my head, I can't touch him. The position stops me from exploring him, and it's frustrating not to get what I want.

My hips reach for him of their own volition while he presses his body tightly against mine. I'm not used to giving someone else control. I fought for the invisible power all my life. Could I relinquish it now?

I drag my mouth from his and raggedly whisper, "I want more." I tug and pull at my restrained hands. If I can just get them loose, I can explore him, devour him, and then leave him. It's the only way.

"I want more, too, and that's why this is going no

further than a kiss. Roxanne, I want us to enjoy each other. I don't want to rush things. We've already waited years; what's another minute, day, or week?"

Seriously? How am I supposed to get through the day with my body pulsing? Frustration overwhelms me, and I scream my annoyance, but instead of the high-pitched squeak I expect, my mouth releases a gravelly, seductive growl.

He drops his body on top of mine, lifting slightly on his elbows to see my face. His weight is a welcome distraction. He releases my hands and takes my head between both of his palms. "We can wait."

"Why are you doing this? It's cruel." I'm not sure if I want to kiss him or punch him.

"Because you're worth it. You jump in the shower, and I'll make breakfast. I'll take you home, and we can hang out at your place for a while. How does that sound?"

"In all honesty, it sounds boring compared to what I'd planned in my head." I pucker my lips, letting them roll into a pout.

His teeth nip and pull on my lower lip before he releases me completely. Losing his body heat has me reaching to pull him back on top of me, but he evades me.

"Go shower, and I'll meet you in the kitchen. I make a killer egg white omelet." He walks to the door. Just before he exits the bedroom, he turns to look at me. "Simply beautiful," is all he says before he walks away.

I let out another frustrated sound. This one comes out sounding like the screech I was expecting. The low rumble of Bobby's laughter follows him down the hallway.

I steady my breath. Maintaining control is impossible if I can't get oxygen to my confused brain. After several slow inhales and ragged exhales, I roll out of bed and pad my way to the bathroom.

His space is tidy, and though his decorating is nothing to write home about, the essentials are present. I turn on the shower and wait for the water to heat. Opening his medicine chest, I inspect the nearly empty shelves. Nothing but a razor, shaving cream, deodorant, and cologne take up residence in the cabinet. One spritz of his cologne has me panting. He may be in the other room, but his scent is with me. I inhale him. He's inside me.

The fragrance is a mix of citrus and something pine-like. It's fresh and outdoorsy. I place it on the counter and strip naked. In the center of the bathroom, his scent surrounds me.

He should package and market the skills he used to seduce me. His was no simple kiss. He's a master of seductive espionage. Every caress, every tingle, every word was a means to get inside my head and my heart. Bobby Anderson is in a league of his own.

I stand under the hot running water, letting it flow over me. His shower gel smells like his cologne. I wash him into my skin. I'll never erase his touch from my body, much less my mind, and now his scent is dancing across my olfactory nerves. He's hijacked my senses.

With the cool air prickling my shower-warmed skin, the heat coursing through my body calms. Bobby is in the kitchen making breakfast. How am I supposed to get through the meal with Mr. Hotness cooking for me? His bare chest will beg for my finger-tips to trail across its hardness.

I drag the T-shirt over my head and pick up a towel from the shelf beside the shower. After towel drying my hair, I wrap it around my waist. There's no way I'm putting day-old underwear back on.

Feeling fresh and clean, I follow the aroma of food to the kitchen. I prop myself against the wall and watch him cook. His muscles flex as he flips the egg mixture in the pan.

"I hope you like mushrooms, onions, and green peppers." He doesn't turn to look at me. He's focused on his task.

"How did you know I was here?" I walked silently across the carpeted floor.

"I can smell the shampoo, and the air changes when you're around. You bring a kind of kinetic energy with you. I can feel you before I see you."

I feel the air change when he's around, too. It started last night when he snuck up behind me. Since then, the hairs have been standing on my arms each time he gets close. It's not the feeling of fear but something electric, like a charge in the air. Can you feel sexual energy?

"I thought you were employing some special detective skills; in actuality, you're presenting some solid culinary skills. Whatever you're making smells great. Did you say egg whites?" Never did an egg white smell so good.

"Yep, I use mostly egg whites because they are light and deliver a punch of protein. I usually mix in veggies or turkey bacon. I made coffee. It's in the pot by the sink if you want a cup. I'm sorry I don't have any cream. I have skim milk, though."

"Yuck, what's the point of using skim milk? You might as well put a splash of water in your coffee and call it done."

"I'll have you know, skim milk is high in calcium and vitamin D. It's good for you and doesn't have all the fat regular milk has. Don't tell me you're a half-and-half girl?" He turns and looks at me. His eyes soften, and his lips curve into a smile. "I'll buy half-and-half for the next time you're here."

"That's so kind of you," I say with a hint of sarcasm. I should save him the trouble by telling him not to bother. I'll never be here again to use it. Our brief reunion is ending. Instead, I embrace the moment. "You're rock solid. Do you eat anything bad for you?" I can vouch for his rock-hard abs as I ran my fingers over them all morning. "Do I need to carb load before I see you?" I know the drill. I know I can't keep him, but the thought of tossing him aside hurts my stomach. My heart pounds painfully in my chest.

"I have to stay fit for work, and I love the way I feel when I eat healthier." He scans my body with hungry eyes. "You look amazing, so you must eat fairly healthy yourself."

I can't look too amazing wearing a jumbo T-shirt and a towel, but I like how his eyes see beyond my apparel. He has the eyes of a hungry man; only food isn't what he desires. I've never felt so sexy in my life. I wish things could be different. Wouldn't it be nice to keep him?

"I walk a lot. I'm also on my feet at my job, so I rarely get time to sit." I pull the towel up my thigh and flex. My legs are muscular. The muscle definition in my calves and thighs is an obvious benefit of not having a car. I never thought of my job as a fitness regimen, but I suppose having a physical job doesn't hurt either.

"Your legs are amazing. Do you run?" He plates up the omelets and takes them to a bar-height table in the corner.

"Yes, I run to the bus stop regularly. Punctuality

is not my strong point. I'm never actually late. I arrive in the nick of time."

"Why don't you have a car?" He grabs two napkins from the center of the table and folds them in half. He places the silverware neatly on the folded paper in front of me.

"I can't afford a car." I place the napkin on my lap and take a bite of my breakfast. I close my eyes and moan as the omelet hits my palate. Nothing has tasted this good in a long time.

"You had a Porsche in high school. What happened to that car?" He looks confused. It's time to set the record straight.

"I had a lot of things in high school, but I didn't have autonomy. I didn't have freedom. I didn't have choices. The price to live my life came in giving up everything my family could provide." I shrug with indifference. It took a long time to get used to living with the basics. My life is simpler now, but simple is good. I used to miss the fancies, but not anymore. Owning my choices is much better than owning Louboutins.

"I'm having a hard time wrapping my head around the concept of you giving up what you had. Things must have been terrible to give up so much."

"You have no idea." I don't want to talk about my family, my dad in particular. The whole subject has the potential to give me indigestion, and this breakfast he made is too good to waste. "I've never eaten an egg white omelet with so much flavor. Where did you learn to cook?" I avoid the conversation, but to his credit, he doesn't push.

"I learned from my mom. All three of us boys had to learn to cook." He pokes his fork into a chunk of egg and brings it up to look at it. "She said it's a skill worth mastering. Do you cook?" He pops the forkful into his mouth. A hopeful expression crosses his face.

"Yes, I learned from the cooks where I've worked over the years. I don't cook healthy fare. I cook whatever sounds good. Most days it's a spicy, red meat concoction that contains an obscene amount of cheese."

"You'll have to cook for me sometime. I love a good artery-clogging meal occasionally."

CHAPTER THREE

With a smile like his, how could I say no? Without thinking, I blurt, "I'd love to." *Shit, did I just volunteer to cook for him?*

"How about your next day off?" He takes a bite of his omelet and waits.

Could I backpedal out of the invite? There has to be a way to walk away without hurting his feelings, a way to bolt without hurting myself. Maybe there's a way to make it work? He's different from the rest.

Hopefully, my fantasy of him is so much bigger and better than reality. That would be the best scenario. I could spend a day or so with him and be over it. Yes, that's a good idea. After a couple of days, we will tire of each other and move on.

"I work Friday through Monday. Tuesdays thru

Thursdays are my days off." I plop the last bite of omelet into my mouth and take our plates to the kitchen sink. The least I can do is clean up.

"So, Tuesday it is. What time should I come to your house? Will six work?"

"Did you just invite yourself to dinner?" I look over my shoulder and find him smiling. He has a beautiful smile. There is a dimple below his right cheek, and I imagine kissing it.

Focus.

It's time for dishes, not fantasies. I turn back to the bubble-filled sink, pretending to be distracted, but my focus is on his answer.

"I suppose I did. I'll bring the wine. You can tell me what you want to cook, and I can bring the ingredients, too, if you like."

"I can afford to fix you dinner. I'm not destitute. I'm merely on a budget."

He laughs. "A Somerville on a budget sounds funny." I turn and scowl at him and then flick the bubbles from my fingers toward him. His laughter rises, and his smile widens.

"You did not just splash dishwater on my face. I know sweet little Roxanne wouldn't do that."

"No, but Roxy would." I reach back and scoop up a handful of water and splatter it against his chest. He's on me in a breath. He pins my hands to my sides while his lips tickle my ear with a whisper.

"Roxy, you are in so much trouble. You know I was just giving you a hard time."

"Bobby, if you were giving me a hard time, I wouldn't be standing here at the sink."

He releases my arms and groans. His lips tease mine with a kiss, and I feel his hardness rise against my stomach before he pushes away.

"I *need* a shower, a cold one," he says as he walks to the bathroom.

I lean on the counter to watch him retreat. This time, the groan I hear comes from my mouth. *Oh, Lord, what the hell have I got myself into?*

Sitting on his couch, I take in my surroundings. His absence allows me to look at his place without distraction. Everything is tidy. His apartment is right out of an IKEA advert. Everything is streamlined and put together. Gray, black, and white are the primary colors. There is a splash of red in his art and throw pillows. For a man's place, it's nice. I pull his T-shirt over my knees. I'd dropped the towel at my feet, not wanting to get his couch wet. In my hand is a magazine called *True Detective*.

"Don't you get enough of this stuff at work?" He approaches me, and the air sizzles. His jeans hug his body, and his shirt leaves nothing to my imagination. And because I know what's under that shirt, I can't get enough of looking at him. Shaking the thought from my brain, I continue my question.

"Don't you want to get as far away from it as possible?"

"No, I love what I do. The magazine is a guilty pleasure. Stories about crime are always so much more interesting than the actual stuff." He slides in next to me and pulls me into his lap. I tuck the shirt around my bottom. Suddenly, I feel self-conscious of my nakedness. It wasn't an issue when he was wearing half an outfit, and I was wearing the other half, but now that he's fully dressed and I'm wearing only a T-shirt, I feel underdressed.

One hand cradles my back while the other rubs my legs from knee to thigh. I lean my head against his shoulder and relinquish my control to him.

"Why are you single, Bobby?" Do I want to know the answer to my question?

"I've been waiting for you."

Oh, he's smooth. If I was younger or the slightest bit naïve, I might fall for his sugary words.

"Right, whatever." I try to sit up, but he pulls me back against his chest and holds me tight. I struggle to free myself, but his hold on me is inescapable. I shouldn't allow him to hold me like this, but he's too strong, and for once, there is a sense of safety within a man's embrace. *He smells divine.* Just a moment longer in his arms can't hurt. "Really, when was the last time you dated someone seriously?"

"Do you want to have this conversation? I believe

in equality in a relationship, Roxanne, and whatever I answer—you answer."

On second thought, I don't want to answer the question, so I let the subject go. My last serious relationship was at least four years ago. I wasn't serious about it, but my family was, which started my push for independence.

"You're welcome to your secrets. I just wanted to understand how a handsome man with a stable job hasn't been snatched up." I relax into his chest and play with the pocket of his cotton shirt.

"It's not a secret. I've been busy. The women I've dated haven't made an impact. Now, I'm picky. I don't want a meaningless affair. I want something more. Not to sound cocky, but if it were just about sex, I could find a hookup any day of the week."

Most men would've sounded arrogant saying it, but after spending the night in his bed, I know he's coming from somewhere more profound, and for me, it's a dangerous place to tread. After spending the night in his bed, just sleeping, I know his statement is accurate. I would've given myself over to him completely. It was always this easy for us. That's what made it perfect. Sadly, the timing is wrong. The circumstances are wrong. The threat is real.

"There is no doubt in my mind you could have anyone. Even I was ripe for the taking." I must have caught him off guard because I'm able to separate myself from his grip and stand up with a push. The rise of the T-shirt gives him a glimpse of my naked bottom. I pull the hem down quickly, squeal, and run to the bedroom.

"You don't have to hide from me. The underwear you had on covered little anyway," he calls from the living room. "If I'd known you were sitting on my lap with nothing underneath, I might not have been so well-behaved."

"I'd like to see your naughty persona," I call from the room. I pick up the blue dress and prepare to put it on.

I know he's there. Even the hair on my body recognizes his presence. It rises with a tingle that courses through my entire being. He's standing right behind me, and every cell is on fire.

"I might like to show you how naughty I can be." His lips brush against the skin at the base of my neck, leaving me weak-kneed and wobbly. His strong arms wrap around my rib cage and pull me tight against him. The weight of my breasts hangs on his arms. Thank goodness he's behind me. I look down at my hard nipples poking against the soft cotton of his shirt. *How embarrassing.* My hair isn't the only thing rising.

"*Mmm.*" The sound slips from my lips. I lean against him and exhale. How can something feel so right and be so wrong? "I need to get home. I have a lot to do between now at my shift. Besides, I can't wear this dress to work." I turn in his arms and press my chest against him. His sharp intake of breath brings some comfort. He wants me as much as I want him. The only problem is, he wants something I can't possibly give him. I can never give myself, not all of me, and he'll settle for nothing less.

"I'm happy your normal attire includes more fabric." He slips his hand down my back and pulls up the shirt. "However, I'm more than pleased to have you wearing next to nothing in my arms." His palm skims over my bare bottom and squeezes it gently. He covers my mouth in a molten kiss, drawing little moans of pleasure from mine as he softly nips at my lower lip before sucking it in to soothe the sting of his bite. I rise on my toes to reciprocate the action. I nip, nibble, and bite his lip, then suck it into my mouth to suckle the soft flesh.

"Roxanne," he groans my name against my lips, and I pull away to look into his eyes——eyes that glow with passion.

I exhale a shaky breath and step out of his embrace. That was possibly the best kiss of my life, and I hate that I have to leave.

He places a chaste kiss on my forehead and walks to his closet.

"Throw these on. You'll swim in them, but it will save you from having to go home in the dress." He hands me a pair of his sweatpants and leaves me to change.

It takes several minutes to catch my breath. I slide my legs one by one into his pants and pull the drawstring tight. The blue dress hangs over the chair in the corner. Looking in the mirror, the girl peering back is a long way off from the girl who wore that sexy blue dress last night. That girl was confident and cocky. The girl in the mirror today is off kilter. Something vulnerable has replaced her self-assured attitude—doubt. I grab the dress and walk out of his room.

He sits comfortably on the couch with his long legs resting on the coffee table. His eyes catch mine. Even though I'm dressed in jumbo workout clothes, he makes me feel sexy.

His head shakes as he blows out a whistle. "Still as hot as ever," he says as he jumps up from the couch. "I want to keep you here, but sadly I can't. You keep reminding me you have a job. I suppose I should get you home." He takes the dress from me. I bend down to pick up my heels and purse, and we head out the front door.

CHAPTER FOUR

Inviting him into my house would have been inviting trouble. We exchanged phone numbers, a passionate kiss, and he left me alone with my thoughts. I had to distance myself from him, but I didn't want to push him away. He intrigues me. He's tall, sexy, and sweet, but so are a multitude of other men.

Sex is what I used men for in the past as a means to an end. The little tingle in my nether regions gets scratched and doesn't require connection or emotion. It's purely physical. One man, one time, one night is my motto. If a guy doesn't stick around, they risk nothing.

I change my clothes into something for work and wait out my time in front of the television. A jewelry store commercial pops up on the screen. The pink diamond reminds me of Emma. Anthony on his knee in front of my roommate was breathtaking.

It's funny how the world often comes full circle. What are the chances I would end up with a roommate who's dating my sister's former fiancé? Emma and Anthony make the perfect couple. My sister Rosanne and Anthony were a mismatch. My family interfered in their relationship. It's the only time my father's meddling worked out for someone —Anthony.

Flipping through the channels, I come across a picture of Emma and Anthony. They are standing in front of the Bellagio Fountains in Las Vegas. They look incredibly happy. Leaning forward, I place my elbows on my knees and focus on the story. The reporter comments on the newly married couple. My mouth drops open. It's no surprise Anthony carted Emma off to Vegas. He was taking no chances she would get away. Laughter bubbles from my chest, and then reality hits me. I may never get a chance to be happy with someone. I don't realize how overwhelmed I feel until I notice the wetness on my cheek from the tear that has escaped my eye.

Bobby's face flashes through my thoughts. Who takes a drunk girl to his home and treats her with the courtesy and kindness of a saint? He was more aggressive in his amorous attempts today, but he never crossed the line. In my mind, there wasn't a line to cross. I wanted him, and he wanted me. Damn him for wanting to take it slowly. The concept of slow is not in my vocabulary. I like the get in, get out, and get lost approach. I've never been able to let my heart rule my decisions. Money, power, and influence have controlled my life from the beginning. Now things are different, and they should be.

The sound of the phone startles me. The name Bobby Anderson flashes across my screen.

"Hello." My voice sounds happy. He has a way of making everything feel perfect.

"Hey, Roxanne. As it's not Tuesday yet, and I'm feeling greedy, I'll come by and have a drink at Trax tonight."

The thought of him at Trax makes me howl with laughter. "That's not a good idea."

"Why not?" Concern seeps into his words.

I envision him walking from the door to the bar. No matter how I work it out in my head, some guy would have his hands all over him. "I work at a gay bar, Bobby. Walking in there would invite all kinds of attention you're not ready for. It's a meat market."

"I'm coming to see you."

"You're sweet, but Trax wouldn't be the ideal location for you. You wouldn't make it to the bar without a few guys hitting on you. Then there are the grabby guys who feel like it's their responsibility to feel you up on your way." There's a moment of silence.

"Hmm, okay, I can see where men grabbing my ass might be uncomfortable. How about I pick you up after work? We could get a late-night snack."

"I don't—"

"I'll be out front waiting." After his abrupt interruption, he hangs up. What the hell just happened?

He's trying to manipulate the situation, but interestingly, it doesn't anger me because I'm just as eager to see him, too. I'm torn between doing the right thing and doing the only thing my heart will allow. My hands run down my outfit, black jeans, black shirt, and black boots. *How depressing.* It's time to revisit my closet. Bobby doesn't make me feel dark with despair. Even after such a short time, not even twenty-four hours, he brings hope. How is that possible?

I rummage through my closet. Hangers that used to hold Chanel and Juicy Couture now hold Forever 21 and Charlotte Russe. It's been a long fall. I find a low-cut, royal-blue T-shirt and slip it on. I freshen up my makeup and spritz on perfume before I head off to work. Pouring drinks and pimping bar snacks has been a means to an end. His simple *I'll be out front waiting,* changes everything from status quo to status go. Every customer I can serve will get me closer to seeing *him* again.

SUNDAY NIGHTS at most bars are slow, but Trax is hopping all the time with all the promotions. Now Sober Sundays are filled with Saturday night revelers who refuse to let the weekend become a memory.

The drink special tonight is the Painus Anus. It's a Tequila drink that contains:

1 Part Tequila

1 Slice of jalapeno pepper

Dash of Hot Sauce

I love this drink. I'm a huge fan of spicy. The hotter, the better. This one doesn't disappoint. Many of the patrons call it the double-dipper—hurts going in, hurts coming out.

"Hey, Roxy." I look up and see Trevor and Chris, who stand at the end of the bar. I race over to hug them. Those two are hands-down my favorite people in the world.

"What are you guys doing here?" I push away and look at them. "This isn't your normal night." They're not Sunday night regulars. They come Fridays, Saturdays, and occasionally on Mondays.

"We came in to get the lowdown on your date last night." Chris waggles his eyebrows. *What a dweeb.* His over-the-top behavior used to catch me off guard. Now I'm used to him. How he ended up with Trevor is a mystery. It's funny how opposites attract.

"I don't kiss and tell." I give them a stern *don't-go-there* look.

"Bullshit, you kissed and told about the firefighter. What is it with you and men in uniform?" Oh... Dan, the fireman. What an awful night that was. The memory makes me shudder.

"I only talked because you guys wouldn't stop asking about his hose. I told you, just to shut you up." I disregard them with a flip of my hand.

"If I remember correctly, by the end of the night, you were begging for more hose, and he had nothing left to give you." Both men break out in laughter, causing every eye in the bar to light upon them. There is something contagious about spontaneous laughter.

"Don't remind me. This is why I'll never kiss and tell again." I pour up their favorite martinis and set them on the counter in front of them. I glance at the clock and realize I have a few hours until Bobby.

Trevor winks at Chris, then asks, "Bobby is a detective, right?" The wink means he's up to no good, but since he's usually the conservative one in the group, I feel safe answering him. If Chris asked, I might have walked away because he's a lecher.

"Yes, he works for Los Angeles County."

"He's a good-looking man, Roxy. Tell us about *his* pistol."

With a roll of my eyes, I leave the men laughing

at their stupid joke. I walk to the other end of the bar to fill a few orders. Another regular comes in. He sits in the dead center of the bar.

"What can I get you?" I look at the man I recognize and try to pick his name from the hundreds floating in my head. "It's Mason, right?" I hope I'm right. Nothing reduces tips faster than forgetting a name.

His face brightens with a smile. "Yes, I'm so happy you remember me."

"I try. It's hard sometimes with so many people. It gets easier if I know something about you. What do you do, Mason? What's your last name?" I look across the bar to make sure everyone has what they need. I have a few minutes to learn something more about Mason.

"Jack is my last name. I teach self-defense classes."

Wow, his statement comes as a surprise. I thought he would say something like construction or long-shoreman. He has a grizzled, outdoorsy look. His skin is weathered, and his hands are gnarled. He's probably younger than he looks, but time hasn't been kind to him. I would guess he's between forty and fifty. Self-defense isn't something I would've imagined.

"Really, like karate?" I wipe the counter in front of him and mentally recite, *Wax on... wax off.*

"I teach Krav Maga. You should come to one of

my classes. You never know when you will have to defend yourself."

The thought of self-defense has crossed my mind a lot lately. When the creeper was stalking the house the last few weeks, I considered the benefit of learning to beat the crap out of someone.

"Where do you hold your classes?" He sits taller in his chair.

"I teach on the weekends at the Baptist Church on the corner of Main and Second Street. Come by, and I'll give you the first class for free."

"I'll think about it." Chris flags me down from the end of the bar. I raise my finger, showing I'll be there soon. After a glance at Mason, I walk away.

"What do you want? I'm not talking about his pistol, his Billy club, or his handcuffs."

Chris's eyes twinkle at the mention of handcuffs. The man is a menace. "I just wanted to know if you saw the news about Emma and Anthony? They got married." Both men look as if they might swoon.

"Yes, I saw the news report earlier. I'm so happy for them. Will she sell the house? Should I look for another place to live?" It just occurred to me that Emma's marriage might mean another move.

"No, she'll keep the house. Maybe she'll ask you to find another roommate. That could be cool."

"Cool is having the house to myself. Emma was like a revolving door as a roommate. She was there, and then she was gone. As a landlord, she's fabulous, but as a friend, she's a superstar. As a roommate, she's just okay. I can't tell you how many days she scared the hell out of me showing up unexpectedly, and given the weirdness of my life, the unexpected is never good. I'm just grateful she worked things out with Anthony." I pour them another drink and make my rounds.

CHAPTER FIVE

I spend the rest of the night hopping from one side of the bar to the next and eventually make my way back to Mason. He's been seated on the same stool all night. If I hadn't had a conversation with him, I would've thought he was creepy, but he seems to be a nice guy.

"Last call," I tell him.

"I'm good. You should come to the class; leaving here so late is risky." He tosses back the rest of his drink and slides the empty glass to me.

"There is always someone to walk me out." That's a lie because I leave the bar alone every night, but no one has mugged me yet.

The thought makes me tremble. He tilts his head and gives me a look that says; *I know you're lying.*

"Tonight, I have a friend meeting me." His eyes narrow to thin slits. "Really, I'll be fine."

"All right, take care of yourself. I'll see you soon." He settles his tab and walks out the door.

As promised, Bobby is standing in front of his silver Mustang when I exit. I love that he wears a suit to work and can rock a pair of frayed Levi's during his off-hours. He looks so sexy. I experience a moment of déjà vu. His smile reminds me of how he looked leaning against my locker every day after school. He focused his eyes on me as if nothing else exists.

He pushes off the car and walks straight toward me. The light in his eyes says he's excited to be here. His exuberance is contagious. Something inside me bursts wide open. He's familiar. He's safe. Whatever it is, I can't resist his warm welcome. Without reservation, I sprint straight to him and throw myself into his arms. Not missing a beat, he lifts me to his waist, where he wraps my legs around him. I'm home.

"Hello to you, too." He supports me by holding my bottom and back. He spins in a circle and then covers my mouth with a kiss. Despite it only being a day, I can't overlook my feelings for him because they never went away. *I won't lose him again.*

"I'm starving. Where are you taking me to eat?" I drop my legs and slide down his lean body.

"Are you positive you're hungry? We could stay here and kiss. I could live off your kisses."

"Hmm, that's a thought." My lips reach for his, but my stomach growls in revolt. The sound echoes through the silence of the night.

"Food it is." He looks at his watch. "At this hour, you have limited choices. It's Denny's or the food truck. Which do you want?"

I weigh my choices. The food truck is greasy and tasty... Denny's is... well, it's Denny's. "Food truck."

He winds his fingers through mine and leads me down the block.

"We're walking? Are you sure that's a smart idea?" I look over my shoulder at his car. It's a nice one and leaving it alone in this neighborhood after they set the drunks loose is risky.

"I'll take care of you, Roxanne. You have nothing to worry about." He pulls his keys from his pocket, points the fob toward his car, and presses the button. The audible *beep-beep* sounds as we continue to walk. "My car is fine. Trust me. It's survived worse neighborhoods."

"Can you call me Roxy? Only my dad calls me Roxanne, and honestly, I don't want any reminders of him when I'm with you." It's a small thing, but Roxy is a different girl than Roxanne. Roxy thinks for herself and does for herself, while Roxanne isn't allowed to think.

"You got it. There's a food truck down the road. They serve a wicked Korean/Mexican hybrid. I love their short-rib tacos."

Anything sounds good right now. I haven't eaten since the egg white omelet this morning.

"You eat greasy short-rib tacos? I can't believe it. Say it isn't so." I pull my hand to my open mouth in mock shock.

"Let's go, they're fabulous, and you'll understand why I put healthy eating on the back burner when it comes to food trucks."

We walk hand in hand for two blocks. The aroma of the food hits me before we turn the corner. The line is at least ten deep, so we wait. I eye every dish that comes past me, and by the time we get to the front of the line, I have a good idea of what I want.

I choose the highly recommended short-rib tacos and green chili fried rice. We get our meals and walk to a nearby wall to sit and eat.

I unwrap the taco, and the aroma rises straight to my nose. The savory smell creates a waterfall in my mouth. "Oh, my God, how did I not know this place was here?" I dive in for my first bite and swear I've tasted heaven. The meat falls apart. The cabbage adds more than crunch. The salsa adds the kick of spice I love and Bobby? Well, he adds warmth to my heart.

"I knew you'd like it. It has everything you love.

It's outside of the norm, it has a kick of spice, and it's unexpected."

Comfortable silence surrounds us. Happy just being, we sit and watch the night and the people who pass by. The darkness brings out the crazies, as proven by the guy wearing roller blades, a red Speedo, and a Superman cape.

"Why did you become a police detective?" I shift my position, so I'm facing him. Pulling my legs up in front of me, I hug them to my chest.

He stalls for a moment. His face takes on a thoughtful look. "I'm not sure I want to tell you the truth." He cocks his head to the side and grins.

I push him with my foot, almost unseating him from his perch on the wall.

"Now you have to tell me."

He grabs my calves and pulls my legs forward, forcing me to scoot closer to him. The angle throws me off-balance. His arms wrap around me, and I feel secure again.

"Do you remember the show *Murder She Wrote*? It starred Angela Lansbury." With his lips quirked to the side, he stares me down, almost challenging me to make fun of him.

"Yes, I've seen the show. She was a writer who found herself in the middle of trouble all the time. Wasn't that on decades ago?"

"Yes, but that is the beauty of cable. What's old can be new."

"All right, what about it?"

"It's what made me want to be a detective. I watched Jessica Fletcher solve crimes year after year. It intrigued me. My mom would say I was obsessed. I never missed an episode." He shrugs his shoulders as if that makes complete sense. Men, always short on words and details. "What about you? What made you want to be a bartender?"

"Don't change the subject on me. You had a crush on Jessica Fletcher, admit it." I cup his cheeks in both hands and turn his head, so he's looking straight at me.

"No, a crush is something I have on you—right here, right now. What I had for Jessica's character was pure admiration. She always got her man. Now back to you. Don't tell me your inspiration was Tom Cruise in *Cocktail*?" He moves forward and gives me a peck on the lips.

Did he just say he had a crush on me? Given how keen he is to pursue me now, maybe those feelings haven't changed. I should put an end to this craziness before he possibly gets hurt. Before *I* get hurt.

"Listen, we can't do this. I can't be with you. It was a great date, but I can't let it go any further. I'm sorry." I hop off the wall and hurry in the car's direction.

"Wait up, Roxy. What the hell?" With his long gait, it doesn't take him but a second to catch up and pull me to a stop. Spinning me around, he holds me in place with his hands on my shoulders. "Tell me what's going on. I'm no Jessica Fletcher, but I can tell there is a mystery surrounding you." He turns my face toward the streetlight. "I won't let you push me away. Your eyes tell me you feel like I do. Your kisses tell me you want me as much as I want you." He presses his thumb against my cheek to catch the tear falling. "You wouldn't shed a tear if you didn't care."

Breathe.

Breathe.

Breathe, damn it.

Nearly a decade of sorrow wells up inside me. Every heartache, every injustice, every missed opportunity comes back to claim a piece of me. I was crazy to bottle up my emotions. Avoidance is a useless tactic. It takes a great deal of energy to erect an emotional fortress and took Bobby no time to destroy it. His very presence reminds me how a world full of pain and suffering can be soothed by the smile and touch of a man—the *right* man.

Every caress has weakened my structure. Every kiss is undermining my foundation. One simple sentence, *I have a crush on you*, and everything came crashing down.

How I ended up on my knees in front of him, I

don't know, but I lie in a puddle of emotions before him. He pulls me into his arms and carries me to the bus stop bench to sit. He cradles me on his lap, where I cry into his shirt. He says nothing, but his willingness to hold me says so much. His gentle caress smooths out the creases of my wrinkled life.

"I'm sorry, I don't know what just happened. I never cry." I bury my head in his chest, and at that moment, I've never felt so safe.

"It's time you let go. You must have gallons of unshed tears stored away. There's no shame in them because everyone cries. Let's get you home. I'm coming in, and we're going to talk." He didn't ask, and I didn't care.

I hold tight, hoping we can stay in this moment for a few seconds longer. When I tell him what I have to, there will be no other moments like this.

He slides me off his lap, but he doesn't let me go. His arm drapes over my shoulders to pull me close to his body. We round the corner glued to each other's side. The uneven tilt of the car sends my heart plummeting.

It doesn't take a detective to see the slashed tire. I reach out for something steady as dizziness threatens to bring me down to my knees. A flash of anger gives me a jarring thump in my gut, and I bolt upright and firm my stance.

Not this time. I will no longer allow him to win.

I wait for the inevitable cussing to start, so I'm surprised when Bobby laughs. He's unlike any man I've met. Most men would start with a torrent of foul language and end with some kind of physical exclamation, maybe a kick to a tire or a punch to a wall. Bobby laughs.

He pulls the spare tire and jack from the trunk. My mind screams, *Shit, shit, shit.* Once again, my father's reach has no boundaries. My hands thread through my hair. Stamping my feet, I pace the length of the car. A tortured scream rises in my throat, but I swallow it as I try to temper my rage. Growing inside me is a fury I need to control. Setting it loose would end in disaster.

I clear the curb of the disgusting remnants of someone's snack. The beige shells rattle against the asphalt as I kick them from my position next to the car. My fingers tap out the numbers on my phone. I've dialed them before, but I've never pressed send. Tonight, I don't hesitate.

Three rings later, his deep voice answers, "Jack Roos. It's late, so this better be good."

My heart beats erratically as I take a seat on the curb. "Jack, this is Roxy Somerville from high school. Do you still run *News to Use*?"

Silence fills the air as I wait for his reply. Was this a mistake? I should hang up. He probably won't remember me, anyway.

"Holy shit... Roxanne Somerville. What's up, girl?" If we were together, I could imagine him giving me a high five as the pitch of his voice hit estrogen levels. "What happened to you? You just disappeared from the scene."

That's one way to describe it. More accurately, they purged me from the lifestyle.

"That's why I'm calling. I've got a story if you still have an audience. It's time for the truth to be told." I swallow the lump in my throat and wait.

"I'm the straight Perez Hilton. I talk. People listen. What do you have for me?"

There is excitement in his voice, and I promise to meet him tomorrow before my shift. Pushing end, I glance at Bobby as he muscles the spare tire into place. For the first time in a long time, I have something to fight for. I *will* fight for him.

The chill of the air eats at my confidence. My shoulders hunch forward, and my knees tuck against my chest. Curled into a tight ball, I wait while he fixes what may be the first minor catastrophe.

CHAPTER SIX

It only takes twenty minutes to change the deflated tire, but It would take a lifetime to heal my deflated heart. I sit near the back of the car and wait.

He throws the flat tire into the trunk and reaches down to tousle my hair. My tired eyes rise to meet his.

"Hey, don't worry."

He pulls me up into his arms for a hug and walks me to the passenger door. Once I'm settled in my seat, he jogs around the car to enter the driver's side. I take a fortifying breath and talk.

"This is because of me. I deal with this all the time. Anytime anyone shows interest, bad things happen."

My voice fades to a whisper. My unshed tears

burn my eyes. What I need most, I will never have—love. My tormentor has eyes everywhere.

"It's a flat tire. Chances are I ran over a nail." He reaches over and holds my hand. The warmth of his palm seeps through my chilled body. "This has nothing to do with you. People get flat tires, Roxy. Shit, this will be my second this year."

Tears blur the lights of the city, and I blink them back and gulp down the bile rising in my throat. I know differently.

The landscape passes by in a blur. Fifteen minutes later, we are at my house. There is a parking place directly in front of my bungalow, but I beg him to park down the street. I can't face coming out to find another flat tire or something worse.

He takes my hand, but I yank it away. Anyone could be watching. He reaches down and grasps it in his and walks me up the sidewalk to the front door. Shakes consume my body. As my fingers comb through my bag to find my keys, I can't control the anxiety ripping through me.

Is he watching now?

Where is the damn key in this mess of a handbag? Shaking fingers are no match for unlocking the door, so Bobby gently removes them from my hand and adds a sweet kiss to my forehead. I wonder if he thinks I've lost my mind.

Once inside, my tightly held breath escapes my

lungs. He shuts the door and comes to stand behind me. With his chin on my shoulder, he says, "There is nothing to worry about. What has you so shaken up?" His breath tickles my neck. His voice calms my nerves.

"Your flat tire was no accident." My voice rises with each word. Rapid heartbeats threaten to escape my chest. "You're a detective, Bobby. Think. Why choose your car when there were others to pick? Why yours and no one else on the block? It makes little sense." I shrug him off my shoulder and walk to the kitchen. "Mark my words, tomorrow you will take the tire to the shop, and they'll tell you someone has knifed it." Glasses rattle against each other as I pull two tumblers and the scotch from the cabinet. "No way in hell will they tell you it was a nail. Trust me; this is my life." I pour us a drink and lead him to the couch.

"It doesn't matter. It was easy to change. We're both safe, and that's all that counts."

I fall helplessly onto the couch. The soft white cushions fold around me like the arms of a loving mother. I can only imagine what *that* feels like, though. To be embraced by the people who donated their DNA—it's perfect in my mind. The cushions open their arms to envelop another as he sits beside me.

I need to have this conversation. It's painful to

talk about my family, but I owe him the truth.

"It's my dad. This is because of him. I wanted to have some control over my life, but when you're a Somerville, you're born without that right. I fight against his tyranny but always end up in the same place: alone, fearful of any relationships, and struggling." Curled into a ball in the corner of the couch, I continue. "I alienated myself from the family, hoping I could gain some authority over my life and choices." I shake my head and take a fortifying breath to go on. "It was a pipe dream. I wanted to be in charge of where I live, whom I date, but no... when I don't please him, I'm redirected. I find myself evicted for bogus reasons like noise complaints, bad credit scores, or forgotten promises to long-lost relatives. You name it, I've seen it."

"Wait, you're telling me your dad has been sabotaging your life for years because you wouldn't fall in line?"

"The detective gets a gold star."

Because of his brilliant mind, I withhold some other causes of my plight. I'm not ready to tell him everything. How long will it take before he squirms and makes some excuse to exit?

He pulls me to my feet and widens his stance. He's a human pillar of strength. With a gentle tug, I'm in his arms.

"I'm not leaving you. I see in your face you expect me to, but I won't. We'll tackle this together. We have a history, Roxy. I know there's more to your story, but you've had a long day. Let me put you to bed, okay? We can talk more tomorrow." He presses a gentle kiss to my lips. "Can I sleep on your couch?"

Couch? He wants to sleep on the couch? How did we get from waking up together to him sleeping on the couch?

"No. No way. You can sleep in my bed." I roll my eyes at him. There is no way he's sleeping on my couch. I've had him snuggled next to me in bed, and I won't settle for less. "I slept in yours, and you'll sleep in mine." I pull him toward the hallway and flip the switch to the first door on my right. I look at my un-made bed and slump forward. "Sorry, I'm not pre-pared for a guest."

"It looks great... comfortable."

I look at my room through the eyes of a stranger. A trail of clothes leads to the Kilimanjaro of fabric in the corner, and I imagine I resemble Felix's Oscar or possibly a hoarder. Laughter bubbles up within me at his attempt at nonchalance. This man is too kind, far too kind for me.

He slides his body behind mine and runs his hands down my sides until they reach the bottom edge of my T-shirt. He pulls up, and the cotton drifts over my head. He tosses it on the heap in the corner. I turn and sit on the bed. Lowering himself to his knees, he unzips my boots and slides them off one at a time. Strong fingers rub my tired feet, which causes me to collapse backward and enjoy the delicious sensation.

When was the last time I felt pampered?

His hands slide up my jean-clad legs and come to rest on the zipper of my pants.

Inhale.

Exhale.

Inhale.

My breath stills as the button pops free. Cool air floats across my stomach. The zipper inches down, one tooth at a time. It's a welcome relief to the heat burning its way through my center. Everything about him seduces me.

I pat the mattress beside me. "It's very comfy. I'm glad you're going to join me." I could get used to him lying beside me, over me, beneath me.

One night, that's all you get, I remind myself. *Tomorrow, I will have to let him go.*

"Hmm, well… here's the problem. There's one issue I need to clear up before we move forward."

"What's that?" I murmur.

"I want to be with you, Roxy. I don't want you thinking about the consequences of being with me. I don't want you thinking up a way to get rid of me in the morning."

I need to add mind reader to his talents.

"Control is an illusion. The only thing you can control is the moment you're in right now. How do you want this moment to go? Do you want to put your pajamas on and climb into bed, or do you want to explore this thing we have together?" His eyes slowly undress me. "I'm not afraid of your father, so tell me what *you* want."

I lean up on my elbows to look at him. Have I ever been asked that question before? What I want? Sincerity and determination are written all over his face. If I tried to sleep, I'm sure he'd bundle me up and tuck me into bed.

The problem is, I want him, but I feel the need to protect him. He may not fear my father, but I know what my father is capable of, and it scares the shit out of me.

The words from my mouth flow like water downstream. "I want this, too. I feel like life has given me a chance to go back and right the wrongs of yesterday. You and I should've dated Bobby. We should've already explored this thing."

"Would have—should have—could have... we are in control of this moment, so I say, let's explore."

He shimmies my pants down my legs and tosses them to the side. Hot, hungry eyes take in my scantily clad body. Dressed in lace underwear, a bead of sweat forms on my brow.

"Let's. Our time is long overdue." I swipe at the

perspiration building on my forehead.

"God, you're beautiful. When we were kids, I used to love Spirit Fridays." Long fingers slide up my bare leg. His touch stops at my knee, but the sensation races to my sex. "All the cheerleaders would dress in their uniforms. I swear your skirt was shorter than the rest of the squad." The palm of his hand slides up my thigh. "I failed Spanish class because I couldn't keep my eyes off your legs."

I giggle at the memory. He sat two seats to my right and was terrible at Spanish. "Venga, sexy, te quiero," I say with my best accent.

"I have no idea what you just said, but it sounds incredibly sexy." He climbs fully clothed up my nearly naked body.

"The loose translation is, 'Come here, sexy, I want you.'"

I pull his T-shirt from his jeans and slide my hands underneath to feel his skin against my fingertips.

"I'm here. What are you going to do with me?"

What will I do with him? If I proceed, I will not let him go. I've known since the ninth grade he is special. His smile and laugh are made for me. His voice vibrates at the perfect pitch to touch my soul. Those things would be enough for most, but it's how he is always so unconditional with everything, from time to love, that sealed my heart to his.

Rather than express myself with words, I try to convey my desires through action. My hands slide under his shirt, raising it above his head. *Yep, his chest is just as fabulous as it was this morning.* It begs to be touched. The button on his jeans pops open with little resistance. I need to get his pants off, so we will be on even footing.

His body weight shifts as he stands. At the foot of the bed, he pulls off his shoes, socks, and pants in record time. He slides beside me. The mattress sinks under his weight. Face-to-face, his long body stretches from the headboard to the foot of the bed. There's not an inch to spare.

Inhaling sharply, I take in the sight of him. The total package is impressive, but the bulge in his briefs makes my jaw drop.

"Think back to the day you were sitting in the lunchroom during our freshman year, and I 'accidentally' poured my chocolate milk on you. Well, I would do it all over again, so I could lick it off right now."

"Hmm, the idea has merit. Should I run to the store to get chocolate milk?" His voice is playful, but something tells me if I said yes, he'd go.

"No, I'm just as interested in tasting you without chocolate." I rise and straddle him. Nails scrape down his chest. My fingers come to rest on the elastic waist of his black boxer briefs. A moment of clarity swims in my head. "Do you have a condom?" I ease my fingers along the waistband of his underwear. The pads brush across the coarse hairs hidden beneath.

Bobby groans. "Damn it." His hands run through his hair, and a loud, frustrated growl escapes his mouth.

"I'll take that as a no, 'Grr.'" I mimic his groan of frustration. If guys get blue balls from sexual frustration, what do girls get?

"You're not on birth control?" There's a surprise in his voice.

"No, I'm not sexually active. There hasn't been a need. What's your excuse for not having a condom?" My question comes out clipped, almost accusatory.

"I could be a smart ass and say I'm out due to high demand, but I haven't been interested in anyone enough to stock my wallet."

It pleases me to know he hasn't been with anyone for a while.

"Well, lover boy, it looks like we'll have to get creative."

I crawl up his body and run my lips around the lobe of his ear. My tongue slips down his neck to pull at the skin on the right side. Sucking gently, I pull it between my lips. The thump of his heart beats in the artery against my mouth. Incoherent mumbles seep through the pillow. I leave the hollow of his neck and trail kisses down his chest. Just as I shimmy down to his briefs, he pulls me up and holds me tight.

"It will kill me to say this, but we can't do this tonight. I don't want to do things halfway with you. I want it to be perfect. I didn't come to the bar hoping we would somehow fall into bed together. I'm happy you want me, but this has to be special. Finding each other again is extraordinary. It deserves a defining moment."

Special? Perfect? He can't do this tonight? *What?* As much as I am thankful—kind of—for his thoughtfulness, I'm horny, and he's hot. His hands run up my sides and graze the edge of my breasts. Goose bumps erupt in the wake of his fingers, and my body is screaming for more. More of him. Sex with *him*. The sensation leaves me dizzy. As if letting me down slowly is his intention, he leans in and kisses me softly, yet with obvious want. Or was that the groan that accompanied it? Who knew Bobby could kiss so sweetly?

"I have to be up in a few hours. Some of us work a traditional schedule." He gives me a seductive wink. "But I don't want to leave your side. I want to know if you feel the same way. Roxy, I want to make love to you more than anything, but I am prepared to wait. To come prepared. This is too important to me to screw up."

CHAPTER SEVEN

My mind races through the words again, *too important, feel the same way, come prepared.*

"Are you leaving me?" Will he get up, get dressed, and walk out? I'm a quivering mess. *What happened to one night?* Love 'em, leave 'em, let 'em go. That's the way it's supposed to be. Bobby has come back into my life, and everything has changed.

"No, I'm going to snuggle up behind you and hold you in my arms. It's my new favorite place to be. However, that will change the minute I settle between your legs."

Disappointed the night won't come to the close I expected, I shiver at the thought of him pressed between my thighs. I dip my head to the side, weighing the merit of his statement. I'll have to be happy wrapped in his arms for the night.

"I'm holding you to Tuesday night." My words throw down a challenge.

"I promise to deliver a night you'll never forget."

He pulls me from the bed and guides me to the bathroom to get ready for sleep. Once in bed, he inches my body into the curve of his. For just a moment, I pretend all is right in the world. I stare at the football on my dresser. My eyes become heavy as sleep pulls me under.

THE TWEET of birds floats in the air, the sound pure and happy. I roll over, hoping to find Bobby sleeping peacefully beside me. The sun is shining in my heart. I reach across the bed, groping for his warm body, but come up empty-handed. Disappointment floods my system. My ears tune in to the surrounding silence, but I only hear chirping birds. I stretch my body, and with one push, I'm on my feet and moving toward the bathroom. A glance at the clock tells me all I need to know. It's ten o'clock, and he's been at work for hours. Did he kiss me goodbye?

I trudge into the kitchen for coffee and find a cup next to a pot already set up to brew. A tented note sits beside it.

I could've stayed next to you all day. I'm sorry I had to leave for work. Text me when you get up. Coffee is ready to brew. You need to shop for groceries. You have nothing to eat except for leftovers of an inde-terminable expiration date and a six-pack of soda. I already miss you.

With affection,

Bobby

Feeling giddy for the first time in years, I hold the note to my chest and wiggle my body from top to bottom. I press the brew button and go in search of my phone and find it on the nightstand.

Lying in my pajamas on my big empty bed, I take a selfie and send him a message.

What's missing from this picture?

Seconds later, my phone chimes.

Me. Naked. Prepared for anything.

Last night's amorous adventure ended prematurely because of our lack of preparation. Any other man would have taken what I offered without a second thought. Bobby wanted something more. He was always different that way. He's the type of man to revere a woman, to see her as a whole person, not just a sum of her few worthy parts. I had intended to have my one night and then set him free. But could I even do that now—set him free? Something tells me it would be nearly impossible.

Don't beat yourself up for not having a condom. It

was nice having you with me all night without the complications of sex.

Is sex with you complicated?

If I tell him yes, will he run? Everything about me is complicated. I want him to leave, and yet I fear he will. I need to get my head on straight.

I'm a Somerville. Need I say more?

I'm not afraid of your daddy, Roxy. He can't scare me away.

We'll see.

We'll talk about this later. I have to go to a meeting, but I'll pick you up tomorrow at five thirty for dinner.

I thought I was cooking.

Nope, you're enjoying it. Dress casual.

Casual, I can do. My closet is full of jeans and cotton shirts. They're a far cry from the Prada and Chanel I wore as a teen. The only elegant item I have is Emma's blue dress. I pull it from the closet and hang it from my curtain rod. I will take it to the dry cleaners on Wednesday.

Looking around the room, it's clear that a good cleaning is in order. If we are going to have a romantic evening, I want something other than an unmade bed and a corner piled high with dirty laundry to greet him. I straighten the house and set the scene. An hour later, I'm climbing off the bus and walking into the office of News to Use.

Jack greets me in the lobby and gives me a once-over.

"What the hell happened to you?"

I'm taken aback by his examination and declaration. My jeans and T-shirt are up to date, and I'm positive I haven't committed any apparel errors. I've seen a few fashion rejects, and I'm not one. My accessorizing is lacking, but I'm on my way to work.

"Life—life happened to me. Listen, I only have thirty minutes because I have to be at work. Shall we get started?"

Precisely thirty minutes later, I leave Jack with his jaw hanging open and his hands on his head. I climb on the bus feeling light and free. Finally, I've stepped into my own shoes. Thirty minutes after that, I hop off the bus with a feeling of dread. A little voice in my head screams, *You made a huge mistake,* but I shake away the sense of fear threatening to engulf me. What's done, is done. I did it. I'll own it.

Martini Mondays are always busy. By seven o'clock, the bar is hopping, and any second thoughts about telling the press about my family are long forgotten. Chris and Trevor sit at one end of the bar while Mason sits in the middle. The rest of the seats are filled with regulars.

"Hey, Mason, what's your poison tonight?"

I eye the man with a hint of curiosity. He's been

showing up a lot lately, but he never hooks up with anyone. He's not your average gay man. He's rugged, steroid-infused, socially awkward, and maybe even a tad shy.

"I'll take a scotch on the rocks."

I lay down a cocktail napkin in front of him and stare as he folds it into a flower. He sets the origami creation in front of me. *Definitely gay.*

"A flower, for me?" I set his scotch on the rocks in front of him and pick up the paper flower.

"It's not just any flower. It's a lotus flower, and it has a significant meaning."

I tilt my head in question. Any opportunity to ask more about the symbolism is denied when several men approach the bar.

"I'll be right back."

I hustle to the end of the bar and fill orders for two dirty martinis, two cosmopolitans, and four vodka martinis with a twist. Chris grabs me before I can make it back to Mason.

"The newlyweds are back." He gushes with excitement. He tells me Emma and Anthony stopped by the bank to say hello. "I bet she's already knocked up. If it's up to Anthony, he'll keep her pregnant for the next several years."

Emma sporting a round belly makes me smile. I'll never wear the blue dress again if Chris's predictions come to fruition. Ugh... parenthood. The thought makes my skin crawl. Is lousy parenting hereditary? I hope not.

"I'm so happy for her. She is one of the nicest girls I know besides Kat. How did your sister turn out so good?" I reach up and mess with his perfectly coifed hair. He smacks my hand away. There's one thing I've learned from my years serving Chris: you don't mess with his hair or his shoes. "What happened to you?"

With a dismissive swing of his hand, he replies, "I was holding the door when everyone rushed in to get the nice gene. By the time I got to the front of the line, the only things left were snarky and sexy, so I settled for sexy. The problem is, I was in the girl's line, so all the feminine, sexy stuff got shoved into my hot male body, and well, you're aware of the rest. It's a good thing Trevor ended up in the same line. We're kindred spirits."

As if he were summoned, Trevor reaches his hands around Chris's waist and pulls him toward his chest.

Love surrounds me. I feel envious of the people who can choose.

"Get a room," I yell at the two of them as they lock lips.

Men practically making love to one another is an everyday visual occurrence for me. My family would never understand or accept it. The concept of love is foreign to them. To me, it's broad and far-reaching. Your heart should decide, not your father.

I reach into my back pocket and pull out my phone. A smile spreads across my face. Bobby sent me a text saying he's going to bed and will dream of me. I float back to Mason, with thoughts of Bobby in my head.

"All right, I'm back. Tell me about the flower."

I twirl the folded pink napkin in my palm. It's incredible how quickly he could create the flower from a simple cocktail napkin. The folds are done with a surgeon's precision, the mind of a mathematician, and the speed of a ninja.

"Why are you so happy today?" He looks at me like a father looks at a daughter or the way a father should look at his daughter. His eyes fill with curiosity, but his demeanor is fluid and easy.

"Flower first." Picking up his glass, I give him a questioning look that asks, *Do you want one more?* He nods while I pour.

"In Buddhism, the lotus flower is considered pure because it can emerge from murky waters in the morning and remain perfectly clean. The lotus is seen as a sign of rebirth. It breaks the surface of the pond renewed every morning. It's fascinating how the open flower and unopened bud are associated with human traits." He swirls the brown liquid in his glass, lifting it to take a drink. He looks at me over the rim. "The unopened bud represents a folded soul. A soul that can open itself up to the truth." His eyes never leave me as his story unfolds. "It's also symbolic of detachment. Drops of water easily slide off its petals. When I look at you, Roxanne, I see a lotus flower."

I stand there, stumped, and a little creeped out. What's all this about rebirth and soul unfolding?

What the hell does he mean?

"How do I remind you of a lotus flower? Most people close to me would say I'm a thorny rose when I'm at my best, a prickly cactus at my worst. There is nothing soft and pliant about me. As for detached, you might have something there." I point to myself and throw my hands in the air in a hallelujah fashion. I turn to walk away, but his next statement surprises me.

"You're wrong. I'm an expert on people, and you're a lotus. I've been watching you for a while. You want people to think you're a thistle, but you're not. You're educated and well-spoken. You walk around with the air of a Rockefeller, but you're a bartender." He tilts his head in a challenge-me fashion. "You accept everyone, but you embrace no one. Your eyes crave affection." He rocks in his seat as if debating his next sentence. "Someone hurt you, but you'll be okay once you embrace the truth about yourself."

His assessment leaves me speechless. How can this man who blends into the background know so much about my soul? They are simple deductions, but something about his observations makes me feel naked. What is the truth he's referring to?

"You are totally off the mark." I roll my eyes and dismiss his long-winded statement about my being. "I'm not afraid to open my heart to someone. My cheery demeanor is because a wonderful man has reentered my life. He makes me smile." Saying it out loud makes it more real. I like the way it rolls off my tongue.

His expression turns hard, but then a sardonic smile spreads across his face like cold, thick syrup sliding over a pancake. "Tell me about this man from your past."

I dismiss his peculiar manner, despite the slightly queasy feeling I get, and tell him about Bobby. "He's a boy I had a crush on when I was a teenager. He would've been considered 'beneath me.' My family has always been on the controlling side. However, I'm no longer restricted by their control and am making choices for myself. Taking the reins as it were."

"Hmm, control is such a tricky word and has so many meanings. By the sound of it, you're like the lotus, and you're coming out of the mud—you're blooming into a new you, unfolding your soul and emerging pure."

Wonder moved through me as I considered how somcone I've barely said two words to before tonight could be so astute and knowledgeable.

"When you explain it like that, I can see myself as a lotus."

I lean across the bar and place a quick peck on his cheek. It's nice a stranger recognizes something beautiful in me. He pulls back in surprise and laughs.

"Why do you call me Roxanne?" My name tag clearly says Roxy.

"It is Roxanne, right? I just assumed. I'm not a fan of nicknames." He shrugs his shoulders.

"I like to be called Roxy." My fingers rub the engraved name tag stuck to my chest.

"Roxy, okay, no problem."

The rest of the evening zooms by. The clock hands spin through the hours. Each one passing gets me closer to Bobby. Tomorrow is our day, and no one is taking it away from me.

A movement catches my eye as I stumble off the bus, and the dark, looming oak tree shifts in the wind. The branches squeak and groan as the limbs crash into one another. I walk toward the movement, and something firm gives way under my feet.

At a dead stop, I scan the area. One more step forward causes the crunching sound to echo into the night. Everything is louder at three in the morning. Pinpricks pepper my skin, making the goose bumps feel like mountains under my light jacket. I stare intently and wait for movement but see nothing. My heart beats a pounding rhythm in my chest. The only external sounds come from the crack of a weak branch. Internally, the thrumming of my pulse in my ears sounds like thunder. I suck in a breath to fill my empty lungs and berate myself for my silliness. It's just my imagination; there's no one lurking in the shadows. Yet, it is hard to quiet the tension that buzzes through my veins.

Will I ever stop fearing the shadows?

CHAPTER EIGHT

Usually, I sleep soundly. Last night, I tossed and turned the entire night. Finally, I fell into a deep sleep around five in the morning. It doesn't surprise me it's afternoon now. These late nights are a bitch. After brushing my teeth, I plod toward the kitchen, fantasizing about my date. Bobby will definitely be prepared tonight.

The coffeepot still holds day-old coffee. My mind fluctuates between microwaving the old brew and making a new pot. Yesterday, my cup was waiting next to a prepared pot with a lovely note. Today, the house is quiet and lonely. I've never felt this way before. Maybe no one has influenced my feelings as much as Bobby Anderson has. I set up the pot and press brew. Everything in my life is taking on a fresh new feel, and that should include coffee.

With a steaming cup in my hand, I curl up on the couch with my phone. I scroll through my messages. There is one from Emma saying she's back in town and officially Emma Haywood.

A pang of jealousy sweeps through me. Emma married first, but my friend Kat is the next one walking down the aisle. No date has been set since the engagement, but it won't take long for Kat to become Mrs. Damon Noble.

I close my eyes and envision a future, and Bobby's face appears in my mind. It's always been him. Sophomore year, we met weekly for coffee. It was as close to a date as we could come. That first kiss was momentous. The skies opened up, and the angels sang a chorus so beautiful, the melody became the code to unlock my heart. No one since has sung the perfect soul song to crack my internal fortress. It has always been easier to keep every other male at arm's length. Safer for many reasons.

The *beep-beep* of my phone jolts my body into awareness. So caught up in my memories, the sound of the incoming text catches me off guard. I fumble with my phone, almost dropping it on the floor. My heart lurches as I look at the message.

Less than five hours before I get to hold you again.

Bobby

You just made my day. I may actually shave my legs for our date because you are so sweet.

Rox

Are you trying to "Rox" my world?

I contemplate my reply for a moment. I smile and text.

You promised a night to remember, and I'll promise to Rox your socks off. Can't wait until you get here.

Rox

Shit Roxy, you're making it tough to get through the rest of the day. I'm tempted to fake the flu just to get to you sooner.

Bobby

I'll be ready at five thirty. Come prepared, lover boy.

Rox

See you soon.

B

Back at ya.

R

I bring my phone to my lips and kiss the screen. Suddenly energetic, I hop up from the couch and do a silly, happy dance. Life has taken me down a different road this time. I live in a magnificent house, have a good job, and an amazing man is becoming a possibility in my life.

I dance across the hallway to my bedroom, make my bed, tossing all the extra pillows across the top so it looks romantic and put together. The candles are ready, and a lighter is nearby. The scene is set. We can pick up wine later.

I pick through my closet and choose well-fitting blue jeans, a low-cut, pale-pink tunic, and a pair of navy-blue espadrilles. The underwear choices are more limited. I pull out my nicest lace bra and panties and set them on the bed.

Now for the big question: trim or shave? It's a toss-up for me. I'm not texting him to ask. I could imagine his coworkers looking over his shoulder, weighing in on the decision for me to shave or not.

A previous date made a statement about the penis having one eye, and the minute it comes out of their pants, it's blind. So, it probably doesn't matter. With my decision set on neatly trimmed, I start the shower and prep my body for a night to remember. Scrubbed, trimmed, legs shaved and slathered with lotion, I exit the bathroom nearly an hour later.

Wrapped in a towel, I walk into the kitchen and pour myself another cup of coffee. I pick up my phone. Bobby sent another text while I was in the shower.

Getting off early, see you in an hour. I hope you're hungry.
B

The message came in thirty minutes ago. I squeal and run for my bedroom, feeling slightly panicked and excited. Getting off early to come earlier. My heart leaps in excitement, and suddenly butterflies dance in my belly. I have less than thirty minutes to dry my hair and get ready.

In twenty-five minutes, I'm finished. I pace the living room, awaiting his arrival. There is more on the line tonight than any other night I can remember. This could be the start of something different—something more than my typical one-night stand. Something more than my daily loneliness.

When I hear the knock at my door, the pace of my heartbeat pounds out a rhythm that could be the background for any techno group. The deadbolt turns, and my heart leaps for joy. He's here, standing on my porch with a handful of Gerbera daisies and a broad smile. Black jeans cling to his long legs, a light-blue cotton shirt stretches over his divinely chiseled chest.

I need deep breaths to keep me from falling in a heap of goo at his feet. *What the hell is wrong with me?* I stand in the entry and stare at him with a goofy grin on my face.

"Can I come in?" He leans in and grazes my lips with a kiss, further scrambling my mind. "Roxy, you look stunning."

His compliment makes my cheeks burn. I shake

the fog from my brain and finally invite him in. "Thanks. Come in. Wow, you look delicious."

I stand aside so he can enter. His citrus-pine scent wafts past my nostrils, the smell taking me on an olfactory trip down memory lane. I travel from his bed to his shower, to my bed, and now my entryway. He presents me with a bouquet of colorful, happy flowers.

"How did you know these are my favorite?" I take them and walk to the kitchen to put them in water.

"You told me about your favorite things when we used to meet for coffee. Gerbera daisies, chai latte tea, Reese's Peanut Butter Cups, Skittles, and the color pink. How did I do?"

"You must be an awesome detective. Your recall skills are phenomenal." Wow, that was years ago, and he still remembers.

"I retain the important stuff. Things were going so well, and suddenly you turned away and ran. I won't let you do that this time. We had something special then, and I still feel it now. Do you feel it, too?" He pulls me toward him and lifts my chin, so I can't escape his questioning look. "I think you do."

Do I admit to the feelings I'm experiencing, or can I dodge the conversation's seriousness and deflect the discussion? It's only been a few days. *Can I be sure of what I'm feeling?* I chew on my bottom lip as I look into his earnest eyes. I don't have the heart to redirect anything. He deserves the truth. I wasn't allowed to explore what I felt in high school, but I intend to examine the possibilities now. *Screw the consequences.*

"Something is going on between us. It scares the hell out of me because relationships have never gone well for me or those I care about. I'm afraid for you. I'm also afraid for me because you can wound my heart." I'm more honest with him than I've been with anyone. I expose my vulnerability and hope it won't come back to bite me in the ass.

"I'm not afraid, Roxy. I told you earlier. You could've told me in high school. I wouldn't have been afraid then either. It's not in my makeup to fear those types of things. My vulnerability lies in you. You can knock me on my rear. I'm putting my heart in your hands, too, Roxy."

"You, too, lover boy. I don't open myself up to just anyone. I'm making an exception for you. Proceed with care."

He lets go of my chin and bends his body to envelop my mouth. His kiss is thorough. His tongue presses past my lips to tangle with mine. He explores the soft recesses of my warm mouth, pulling a moan from deep inside me. Strong hands thread through my hair to hold me in place. He has plundered my store of good sense with just a kiss and replaced it with wild abandon. My breath pitches and pulls, gulping for air and then feeling as if I've swallowed too much. He removes his lips from mine, leaving me with a feeling of emptiness.

Indecision is written all over his face. There appears to be a war waging inside him. I know the minute it's won. A look of determination settles over his face. His brow relaxes, and his lips soften into a smile.

"It would be so easy to stay and feast on your kisses, but we have a date. This is the date we should've had years ago, and I plan to make it a memorable one. Grab a jacket and let's go before I change my mind."

His long inhale and slow exhale are proof the kiss affected him as much as it did me. He appears to be breathing his way to control. I follow his example and breathe deeply. The oxygen clears my brain, but my body still hums with excitement. I walk to the hall closet, pull out a jacket, and follow him out the door. Sitting in front of my house is his sleek, silver Mustang. He opens the door for me before he runs to the other side and hops in the driver's seat.

"Are you ready?" His tone implies something more than dinner.

With a smile on my face, I clap my hands like a lunatic and say, "Yes." I don't know where we're going, but anywhere is the perfect place if we're to-gether. "Where are we going?"

"You'll see. We were supposed to have a date years ago, but it never happened. This is that date. I had it all planned then, although I had a smaller budget when I was a teen."

"I'm sorry we delayed our date by so many years. I wanted to go then, but I couldn't." I reach my hand across the center console and grab for his. He lets go of the steering wheel and holds mine—this feels right.

"I have some idea of what you went through. Rumors were ripe at school. I know it wasn't personal. I only wish you'd have trusted me to stand up to your dad."

"You were sixteen. You were no match for my father. Maybe it's better this way. We're older and wiser. I feel so blessed Emma tracked you down. I mentioned you in passing, and she did a Jessica Fletcher and found you. That girl is tenacious."

He smiles, most likely at my reference to his childhood idol.

"Too bad she plans to be a billionaire's wife. She has some mad investigative skills. We could use her at the station."

He turns off the interstate and drives toward Santa Monica. It's charming our first date would've been and still will be near the beach.

"Emma works for Anthony Haywood's. I'm independent, so I don't see her caring much about his money. She'll do what she wants. As for the precinct, there's still hope. You'll need to recruit quickly, though; rumor has it, Anthony plans to expand the Haywood family."

"A man on a mission. I like him. I might have to get some lessons on swag from him. He melted her heart with an enormous diamond the other night. Is that what it takes?" His profile can't hide his frown. "I hope you don't place a great deal of importance on money. I don't have any."

"You look like you're doing all right. Let me tell you, if we compared savings accounts, I'm sure yours would be in better shape than mine. Don't get me wrong, I have money, but not a lot." My financial state of affairs is commendable. I have several thousand dollars in the bank, but more importantly, I've been taking care of myself for the last few years. Pride swells inside me. "Don't forget, I left a privileged lifestyle to do what was right for me. Money isn't important to me. We'll never need more than enough." I just put we and a reference to the future in the same sentence. The thought of us having a future gives me warm and fuzzy feelings.

"I certainly have enough. I can afford to take you out whenever you want to go with me." The engine shifts, and the car rumbles as it speeds up. That throaty sound is damn sexy.

"You should be careful with those offers. I might want to go out all the time. Then what?"

What would a steady dose of Bobby be like? Would it always be exciting, or would the newness wear off, eventually? I would like to stick around and find out. If he were going to turn and run, wouldn't he have done it the other night?

"What happened with your tire?" I already know the answer, but I want to see how long it will take him to reveal the truth on his own. Too long. I'm dying to be vindicated.

"It was flat. I got it fixed." His voice is even, controlled.

I reach over and slug him in the shoulder. "I know it was flat, but we had a bet about the cause. You said nail, and I said it was something sinister." I turn in my seat and wait for his reply. The muscles in his jaw tense before he says, "You were right. The tire was slashed. It could have been random. We'll never know." He squeezes my hand softly. "Don't worry about it. It's just a tire."

"I know, but this is how my life goes. It's a tire, a window, a threatening letter. I've seen a job loss, an eviction notice, and trouble with the law. His reach has no limits."

"You think it's your dad? If that's the case, I'll have to visit him. He might not have liked me as a teen, but he has no idea who I am as a man."

He pulls the Mustang in front of an Italian restaurant and hops out. The valet opens my door and helps me exit. I grin at the fact that we are using valet parking. He's taking no chances with his car tonight. He pulls me to his side and walks me into the restaurant.

Once we check in, the receptionist takes us to a private table in the restaurant's rear. Checkered tablecloths dot the landscape, and fragrant garlic and oregano fill the air while subdued lighting and the crooning of Frank Sinatra set the mood. Bobby pulls my chair out, and his lips caress my neck as he helps push me in.

"I hope you like Italian food?"

"I love it." My voice, breathy and wispy, sounds unfamiliar—like something straight out of a fifty's movie.

"Promise me tonight you won't worry about anything. This is about you and me. Okay?"

I agree with him. All I want is this time to be only ours.

It's been twenty-four hours since I told my tale to *News to Use*, and so far, everything is quiet. I wonder if my father has seen the release. Silence can be so unsettling.

CHAPTER NINE

Seated next to me, he looks over my shoulder at the menu—his breath brushes across my bare skin, the nearly invisible hairs standing at attention.

"I highly recommend the tortellini."

His words float over my senses like an exposed electrical current. Who could've known the word "tortellini" could be so stimulating? I repeat the word in my head. *Tor ta lini,* definitely sexier coming from his mouth.

"Is that what you're having?" I browse the menu and try to choose between veal scaloppini and chicken saltimbocca. "I was hoping we could order two things and share them."

"We can do that. I've been known to share some things." He glides his arm over my shoulder and pulls me toward him. "I won't share you, though. I draw the line there. I'm staking my claim to you right now. If you have a problem with that, let me know immediately."

Do I have a problem with him claiming me? He'd be the first person to do so in years. The word "claim" sounds like a declaration. At least that's been my experience throughout the years. Words like "defiant," "selfish," and "bitch" are common in my vernacular. I've been called those words a lot. He speaks of something different—a possession, and a warm, comforting feeling runs through my veins. Somebody cares about me; someone thinks I have value—his name is Bobby Anderson, and I want to be his.

"I'll have the veal scaloppini."

A smile breaks across his face. Not addressing his claim is accepting it. His lips crush against mine and suck the oxygen out of the air. I break away to breathe.

"You don't know what you're up against. I'm telling you, things will get worse. I wouldn't blame you if you cut and run right now. At this point, you've only lost a tire."

I wait for the uncertainty to cross his face. I pull my lower lip between my teeth and gnaw on soft flesh. His face shows no sign of doubt. He looks unfazed as the pad of his thumb brushes across my lower lip. With a gentle tug, he pulls it from between my teeth.

"Ouch, that hurts."

"You nearly chewed a hole through your lip. I'm saving these for later."

His tongue licks across my swollen lip. A cough interrupts our moment. Both of our eyes look up at the impatient server hovering over the table. The man taps his foot and waits with his pen and pad in hand. I laugh. Bobby looks relaxed. He orders dinner for both of us and then returns his attention to me.

"What are you staring at?" I never had anyone pay me much attention, and the awareness is exciting and unsettling.

His eyes twinkle in the candlelight. If eyes could smile, his are Cheshire cat worthy.

"I'm looking at a beautiful woman who should enjoy her date. Instead, she's trying to protect me. I can hold my own, Roxy. Trust me." His tongue slips out to moisten his lips. I would have happily volunteered to lick them myself.

"Oddly enough, I *do* trust you. I don't give my trust easily, so make sure you remain worthy of my confidence."

"I promise to take care of you. Tell me what your father gains from trying to control you."

"You said he wasn't invited on our date. I don't want to talk about him." Grabbing a piece of bread from a basket the server left, I shove a bite into my mouth, making it impossible to talk.

He shakes his head and chuckles. He sees right through my avoidance tactic. Maybe dating a detective isn't a wise choice. He rarely misses a beat.

"I also told you we were going to talk. Once we get to your place, we'll get distracted." His lower lip pulls between his teeth. *Damn sexy*. "So… let's talk now. We have time."

His hand slips below the table and rests on my thigh. The slide of his fingers across my leg is distracting but comforting. His connection gives me the strength to venture into uncomfortable territory.

"Control—he wants to control. I wouldn't date and marry who he wanted me to, so I became persona non grata. It started with him ignoring me. It turned into him denying me things like clothes and allowance. He—"

"This fight you have with your father is about clothes and allowance? That's a petty thing to fight about." His frown shows disappointment. "How long has it been since you've spoken to your family?"

"It's been four years. You didn't listen to the part about him making me date whom he deemed worthy. I wasn't into leering older men. He wanted me to marry a partner. You know, keep it in the family—his real family—the lawyers at the firm." Pushing my seat back, I turn to look him straight in the face. "I refused to bend. First, he stopped paying for college. I got a job as a bartender. He arranged for my apartment lease to expire. I moved into a new place, and he got them to evict me over a noise complaint. Then came the threats on any man who showed interest. The first one lost his job, and the second was mugged in an alleyway. It's always something. Things have been calm for a few months, and then this man started staring at the house I'm living in now."

His eyes rise while his jaw tightens. "What man?"

"It turned out to be Emma's father. He was stalking her before he showed up in person to reassert himself into her life." Some of his coiled tension appears to evaporate.

"Have you seen him since then?" His eyes search mine for the truth.

"No, I thought I glimpsed someone in the shadows last night, but it was my overactive imagination. No one was there." He visibly relaxes. "I'm watching your detective's brain work overtime. What are you thinking?"

"I'm thinking you need to learn how to defend yourself. You also need to meet with your dad, iron things out with him, and let bygones be bygones. You're an adult and can decide who to date and where to live at this point in your life."

"You'd think so, but he wants total control of

everything. I haven't given him what he wants. I've been unpredictable." I smile sweetly.

"What are you up to?" His eyes close to slits as if this will intimidate me into confessing something nefarious.

I bite at the tiny loose piece of skin on my lower lip.

"I may have let *News to Use* ask me some personal questions. I answered honestly, and those answers might shed an unfavorable light on one of the most well-known lawyers in Los Angeles."

"Oh, Roxy, why didn't you talk to me? Do you think exposing him like this will help your cause? He's a lawyer. He might sue the newspaper or even the reporter for defamation of character."

There's that look of disappointment again, and I feel like an errant child.

"You were changing the tire, and I was furious. I won't let him run you off." I blush. In a way, I've now staked claim to him.

"I know you're angry. I've seen you in action. Don't forget, we hung out for years in high school. You can be sweet, but you're also stubborn and relentless. I can see you disagreeing with your dad just to disagree." He shakes his head. "Do you want me to talk to him? Maybe coming from a man, he might be more reasonable. I just wish you'd have talked to me first."

I want to roll my eyes but refrain from the disrespectful act. "No, I'm taking care of it."

"Publicly exposing the situation isn't the same as taking care of it. You should visit your dad."

The server delivers our food, ending the discussion. He pours us a glass of Chianti and leaves us to enjoy our meal. Bobby hands me a drink and picks his up for a toast.

"Here's to a bright future."

"A bright future." I tap his glass and take a sip, wondering how bright it can be.

We eat our meal and talk about life. I pierce one of his tortellini with my fork and place it in my mouth, savoring the flavor of Italian sausage and cheese. Delicious. Next, I prepare a bite of my food to place in his mouth. I slide the fork between his lips.

His eyes roll back as he slowly chews the tender veal. *Hmm, Bobby in ecstasy. I like that look.* We compare notes on music and movies and find out we have a lot in common. Aside from detective shows, he's a massive fan of action and adventure movies. We're both obsessed with all Liam Neeson films.

Hand in hand, we leave the restaurant, full and happy. If the date ended now, I'd consider it perfect. But there's more—lots more. My heart sings with joy at the thought. He guides me to the pier where we make our way to the Ferris wheel. Bobby has a private conversation with the man in charge. After he helps me into the car, it lurches forward, stopping several times to load new passengers. Once everyone is loaded, it makes its circle. At the top, it stops. The cart sways back and forth.

"Look out there, Roxy. Isn't it beautiful?"

I gaze out over the ocean at the glow of lights from distant boats that dot the horizon. The moonlight glimmers off the water—it's peaceful. The wind whips through the car, giving me a chill. As if sensing my need, he immediately wraps his arms around me and pulls me close.

"I feel on top of the world when I'm with you. Life is good, but it's so much better because you're here."

If my heart wasn't in it before, it's fully committed now. The moving of the car startles me, making me grab onto his shirt. I cling to him. We travel through several more rotations before the ride ends.

The operator smiles as we exit. I reach over and give the older man a peck on the cheek. His stall at the top gave me one of the most romantic moments of my life. The least I can do is kiss him.

With our hands intertwined, we walk through the arcade. He shows his pitching skills by winding up and knocking the milk bottles off the table, winning me a small stuffed monkey. We stop at the funnel cake stand and order one to share. By the time we're finished, we're both covered in powdered sugar. A speck of white dots his lip, so I pull him down and lick it clean. Before I can pull away, he drags his lips across mine and down my neck. We cut the kiss short when the carnie tells us to get a room.

We descend the steps to the beach with our fingers once again laced together. I slide my shoes off and hold them in my free hand next to my stuffed animal—the cool sand shifts between my toes. At the water's edge, I roll up my pant legs as Bobby removes his shoes and socks and does the same. We leave our belongings on the dry sand. We race into the water as the tide rolls out and retreats as the waves crash in. Cold water catches our feet, and laughter fills the air as he picks me up and spins me in circles.

"Shall I toss you in?" He swings me toward the water and pretends he will let me go.

"You better not. I swear if you let me go, I'll..." I try to come up with some kind of punishment.

"You'll what?" He holds me close to his chest and lets me slide down his body. I cuddle into the warmth he brings.

"I don't know, but it'll be bad." I laugh at myself for being incapable of a good threat. Hell, being in his arms, I'm barely capable of a clear thought.

"What if I like bad?" He nips at my lips.

"Then I'm the perfect girl for you."

"You're right." He rubs noses with me and swallows me up in a bear hug.

"You are so sweet. I want you, Roxy," he groans as his kiss grazes my lips.

"Hmm, let me think. We can stay here on the beach and kiss like high school kids, or we can go back to my house and pretend we're adults. I vote for home. Let's pick up a bottle of wine on the way."

"Yes, let's go. You have goose bumps." He rubs his hands up and down my arms. "I thought I told you to bring a jacket?"

"I did. It's in the car." The cold isn't causing my goose bumps; his nearness makes my skin rise in anticipation.

"It won't keep you warm if it's in the car."

He presses himself against my back, then wraps his warm arms around me and puts his chin on my head. We stay folded together, both staring at the waves crashing against the sand. The foam of the surf spreads through our toes, and the chill of the water breaks us both out of our private thoughts.

"Shall we head to your house?"

The excitement of the moment stills my heart. I've carried a torch for this man since high school. With our shoes in our hands, we walk through the sand to an empty bench near the sidewalk. He kneels in front of me and wipes the sand from my bare feet before placing my shoes back on. I feel like Cinderella when the glass slipper fits. It's a good thing he has a grip on me because I'm weightless. My heart is buoyant—floating on cloud nine with Bobby. He is light and love rolled into one package.

He puts his shoes and socks on and guides me back to valet parking. His eyes scan the car as the valet pulls it to the curb. Relief appears to wash over his face as it has come back in one piece. He helps me enter before getting himself buckled into the driver's side.

"You worried your car would hobble out of the garage, didn't you?" I giggle at the image my mind has created, picturing his shiny silver Mustang bandaged and limping to the curb. I have to stop watching animated movies.

"In all honesty, I wasn't sure, especially since you told me you went public with some of your family's dirty laundry. What exactly did you say?" He puts the car in drive and heads toward home.

"I just told him the perfect life my dad paints for the public is anything but the truth. If you step out of line, you're out. If you fail to comply, you get punished." I pull out my phone and load up the website for *News to Use*. Considering Jack's response to my visit yesterday, he's probably already dished up something juicy to print. My screen loads and the headline reads,

Life at the Top Isn't Always so Sweet—Poor Little Rich Girl.

The article outlines how my father disowned me for not wanting to marry a man twenty years my senior. How little by little he sabotaged my life and how he continues to muscle me into submission by threats and violence. The headline comes across as condescending, but the meat of the piece is spot on.

I read the entire article to Bobby. Silence fills the air as we both chew on the information posted for the world to see. I consider the report and don't find fault in a single word. I reported my side of the story without embellishment. Will my father step up and tell his version of the truth, or will he try to paint a different picture?

CHAPTER TEN

After a quick trip to the neighborhood liquor store, we arrive at the house. Being ever the gentleman, he walks around the car to open my door and help me exit. *Thudum, thudum, thudum,* my runaway heart races. Will my heart arrive at the door before I do?

I glance up the sidewalk to the dark porch. Did I forget to turn the light on? I swear my finger toggled the switch as we walked out the door. Maybe the bulb burned out.

My fingers search the bottom of my purse. I feel the notched ridge of the lone key in the corner. Trying to find the keyhole in the dark isn't an easy task. This is the story of my life, always in the dark, searching for something. Sadly, unlocking a door is symbolic of my existence.

"Hey, before we go in, I want you to know this only goes as far as you're comfortable. The minute you want to stop, we stop." His statement is so Bobby. He's always so calm, whether it's on the football field or on my front porch. What would it take to make him squirm? Just once, I'd like to see him lose control.

"I'm all in lover boy. Let's go."

My heart pounds in my chest. Courage doesn't drive me. My desire is precipitated by the need to do something, enjoy something, control something.

"Lover boy, huh? Is that going to be my nickname?" Still, on the doorstep, he runs his lips up my neck to the lobe of my ear.

"It depends. Can you live up to it? It's a big undertaking."

On my tiptoes, I kiss his mouth, pulling his bottom lip between my teeth, and bite down. The pressure isn't enough to hurt, just enough to remind him I've been there.

"Didn't I feed you enough?" He pulls his lower lip between his teeth. The action is so damn sexy.

"I hunger for something different right now." I run my hand down his body, skimming over his hardened nipple. An audible groan tumbles from his lips.

"Open the door, Roxy; otherwise, I might take you here on the doorstep." His tight voice now has an edge.

My chest swells with something akin to pride. To

unsettle Mr. Self-restraint is quite an accomplish-
ment. I turn the knob and push the door, but it
catches on something and stops.

"That's weird. There isn't anything in front of
the door." I push again, but it moves marginally. "We
walked out this door."

"Let me try to open it." I move to the side and let
him muscle his way into the house. The unmistak-
able sound of broken glass crunched under his feet.
"Stay here. Get in my car and lock the door." He
pulls the keys from his pocket and hands them
to me.

"Now, Roxy."

His no-nonsense voice sends me scurrying to the
car. I climb in, lock the door, and wait. I follow his
progress through the house as the lights glow and dim
behind the semi-opaque window treatments. Several
minutes later, flashing lights draw my attention away
from the bungalow.

*Wow, there's a lot of stuff going on in the neigh-
borhood tonight.*

Black-and-whites sandwich me in. Bobby greets
the officers like it's a high school reunion. It's got to
be bad if he called for reinforcements.

A surge of adrenaline runs through my veins.
The thrumming is so loud that all I can hear is
the *swoosh, swoosh, swoosh* of blood in my ears. My
heart clunks to the floorboard the minute Bobby

comes to the window. I didn't see him leave the officers and approach.

Click, I unlock the door and hop out. "What's going on?" My eyes move around him to watch the officers enter my home. "Have I been robbed?"

He rubs his chin between his thumb and index finger. A thoughtful look appears on his face. Soft green eyes hold mine. "This wasn't a robbery."

"I want to go in." I turn and walk up the sidewalk. "You're keeping something from me." He reaches for my arm and hauls me back to his side. "What aren't you telling me?"

"You can't go in yet. The officers are investigating." He loosens his grip on my arm. I take a few steps toward the house. "Emma needs to be notified because she owns the place. Can you call her and tell her to come right away?" His request stops me in my tracks.

I stomp back to the car and grab my purse. With my phone in my hand, I punch in the numbers and wait for Emma to answer. After I explain what I can, which is little, Emma says she's on her way. It will be about thirty minutes until she can get here from across town.

I stand in front of Bobby and relay the message. "They live in Malibu. It will take them a bit to drive this way. Do I have to wait for her to arrive before I can go in? Please, tell me something," I plead. My mind races through several possibilities. As far as I know, there could be a dead body in the house. *Oh, God, is there?* "Please tell me there isn't a dead person in my house." My head pitches back. My eyes get wide.

"Come here." He pulls me into his arms and holds me against his chest. "There isn't a body in the house. However, it is a crime of violence, and it appears personal."

"What do you mean, it's personal? What did you find in the house?" Immediately, the interview with *News to Use* comes to mind. I lean back and thump my forehead with the heel of my hand. "It's my dad, right? You think he hired someone to toss the house because I spilled the beans?" I let out a frustrated growl.

"I don't know what to think." He leans over and opens the door to the car. He reaches a long arm into the back seat and takes out my jacket. He folds it around my shoulders, helping me slip my arms into the sleeves. "You have goose bumps." He rubs his hands up and down my arms. The friction creates much-needed comforting warmth.

When something like this happened in the past, I was alone to pick up the pieces. In the past few days, Bobby has proven he plans to stay by my side. It's amazing how peaceful that makes me feel. I follow his line of vision to the house. His face looks calm and controlled, but his body rigid and stiff. His soft words relax my threadbare nerves, but he appears to be tethering his restraint by a hair. I'm not so sure I want to see him lose control.

"Is it bad?" I lift my head to look into the sea of green. His eyes hold the truth. They stare at the house, then back to me.

"It's bad." *At least he's honest.* "You can't stay here." His hand splays across my back and pulls me into his frame. If we get any closer, we'll be wearing the same shirt.

It must be terrible if I can't stay. Emma will be so upset because she loves this house. This is all my fault.

It may take me a lifetime to pay her back for whatever damage is done. How does everything get so out of hand? Sorrow rises to choke me. Sometimes, it's too much to deal with alone.

"What am I supposed to do?"

As if reading my mind, he says, "You're not alone. I'm here, and I'm not going anywhere."

It feels good to have someone at my side, if only for the moment. It feels good to have him with me. Sadly, it's only a matter of time before it will become too much. Years have been stolen from me. A week ago, I would've shrugged my shoulders and moved on —started again. How many times do I have to begin again? The thought of not having him crushes my heart. The pain is palpable and the loss makes me whimper.

I need a rewind button. If I had one, I'd go back to the day at the coffee shop and say yes instead of no. To be his girlfriend would be my greatest joy.

A spark of fire has been building up over the years, and it's smoldering. Little flickers of flame burn out my doubt. Gritting my teeth, I hold on to the heat of anger. It's better to feel fury than defeat.

"I'm not giving you up." *Shit, did I say that out loud?*

"You don't have to. Once we get back into the house, we'll grab whatever is salvageable, and you'll come home with me. You belong with me. Haven't we always known, Firefly?" The thought is sobering.

Even after he was long gone, his influence was always there. I chose men with his looks. Brown hair and green eyes looked back at me, but those men were temporary solutions to a long-term problem. Bobby has always been my problem, or maybe he's the solution.

Two words grab my attention. The first is "salvageable," and the second is "belong." "Salvageable? Really? How bad is it?" I take a deep breath and exhale slowly, my mouth forming a tight "O" as the air pushes past my lips.

"I won't lie to you. It'll surprise me if there's anything you can take out of there. You may be wearing my clothes tomorrow." If his smile is an indicator, he finds the possibility appealing, but there's concern written on his carefully masked face.

I spent my high school years studying him. When I couldn't have him physically, I took him anyway, even if it was only in my mind. I memorized every dimple, every speck of gold in his eyes, and every curve of his smile.

"Where did you go after high school?" My question might come from left field, but I recall the pain of graduating and never seeing him again. It was like he disappeared off the face of the earth.

"You're funny. Your home is destroyed, and you want to talk about what I did after high school." He leans against the Mustang and pulls me against him. We both stand with our eyes glued to the house. His chin comes to rest on my shoulder. His breath tickles my ear.

"Humor me, or at least distract me."

"I can think of all kinds of ways to distract you, Firefly, but for now, I'll humor you."

Firefly? Where did that come from?

"Good. Tell me what happened between then and now?"

CHAPTER ELEVEN

I relax my body into his. Even though he stands nearly a foot taller, our bodies fit perfectly together. I tuck up under his chin with the precision of a laser-cut puzzle piece.

"I went to work for a private investigator while I attended college. I got my degree in criminal justice from UC Irvine. I was nearby the whole time." His arms wrap tightly around my center. "I focused on school and getting hired by the Los Angeles County Police Department."

"I'm glad you got to pursue your dream. What did you do for the PI?"

"Mostly paperwork. I filed a lot of paperwork." He lets out a low grumble.

"Sounds boring."

"It was, but it was a paycheck. What would you do if you could do anything? I know you were going to get a law degree, but it's clear that law wasn't your choice."

I sink deeper into his embrace. The gentle sweep of his hands on my arms soothes my nerves. I haven't given my future a lot of thought. But in his arms, I see possibilities.

I'm embarrassed to tell him all I want in life is to be held in his arms, but my current aspirations halt right there. It's not a sound decision to have your biggest dream controlled by one man. To be loved by him would be my be-all and end-all. Everything else is meaningless.

He's waiting for an answer. I tell him a few things I might find fun to do.

"I like to bartend, but I don't like the hours. I like to cook, but I haven't been to culinary school. I have a head for numbers."

After a minute of contemplation, I say, "I would go into restaurant management or open a culinary school for kids. Something creative would be fun. Managing a place like Anthony Haywood's would be awesome."

"Since his wife is your landlord and friend, I bet you have the perfect connection for advice and consideration. You should talk to him about doing an internship."

As if summoned by the conversation, Anthony and Emma step out of a sports car and survey the area. The police cars are still out front, lights flashing. Bobby pushes off the car and transfers my body to his left side. We meet the couple midway. Everyone smiles and says hello despite the less than hospitable situation looming in front of them.

Emma reaches out to me. "Are you okay, Roxy? I'm sorry this happened."

She's sorry? That's a funny thing to say. I feel responsible for whatever lay inside. I decide to tackle that conversation with Emma alone. Most pressing is the ability to go inside and survey the damage.

The officers walk out the front door. Bobby draws everyone's attention by clearing his throat. "It looks like they're going to turn it over to us. Let me just confirm we have the all-clear to enter." He disappears up the walkway and talks to the officers.

"You look happy, Emma." I look at my friend's healthy glow. Even with all the crap happening, she appears in good spirits, almost beaming. Marrying Anthony has brought peace to her life. "Let me look at your wedding ring."

Emma proudly presents her hand. Her LED smile battles her ring for attention. A simple gold band sits next to the enormous pink diamond. With a gentle twist, she exposes the tattoo hiding beneath the basic band. Beautiful script circles her finger. It says, *Only Anthony*.

"Isn't it great? Anthony's tattoo says, *Emma Always*. It hurt like hell when we did it, but it's forever."

The permanent bands speak to their commitment. Their journey to love wasn't easy, but they got there, nonetheless.

I rub my bare ring finger. Bobby's been the one since ninth grade. Will it be the same for us? One thing is for sure, I'm not into pain, and I'm not tattooing my body. I have a few piercings—I can remove those—but I can't take off ink—not easily, anyway. "Permanent" hasn't been in my vocabulary for a long time.

Bobby approaches the group. "All right, we can head in, but I have to warn you, it's not pretty. There are lots of messages around the house. They aren't pleasant to look at. Maybe Anthony and I should go in and deal with it."

Emma and I scream, "*No*," at the same time. There is no way we'll be left behind.

"Bobby, I don't call my woman Red for nothing. She has a fiery hot temper, just like a sizzling ember. Roxy's isn't much tamer. You better step aside and let them through." Anthony stands aside like the smart man he is and lets Emma and me lead the way.

"Son of a bitch," Emma calls out. "Stupid assholes."

I stand off to the side, looking at the damage. Scrawled across the walls are the words "whore," "slut," and "bitch." The house is unrecognizable. Glass covers the once shiny wood floors—feathers floating in the air at the slightest movement. The down filling of the sofa was set free through multiple slashes in the cushions, and they swiped all the shelves clean. Their contents lay broken on the floor. Room by room, we tread carefully through the house, and step-by-step, I feel nausea tempting to over-whelm me. The bitter bile spills onto my taste buds, threatening to gag me, and it reminds me that my life is anything but sweet.

A gasp from Emma startles me as we walk into my room. "I'm so sorry. This is all my fault." Emma's eyes bulge with rage. Her red hair seems to ignite around her head.

"How's this your fault?" I clasp Emma's hands in mine. Tears spring to my eyes as I survey the damage. "It's my fault. This is because of the problems be-tween my father and me." Anthony's eyes move to my face at the mention of my father. He's had some run-ins with Mr. Somerville.

"Roxy, I just took the most eligible bachelor off the market. I ran an escort service—a legitimate one, mind you—but some people still considered me a whore. This is about me. Did you see the words carved into the walls? 'Bitch', 'whore', 'slut', they were meant for me. I own everything except what's in your bedroom, and it's all been destroyed."

Emma may live in Malibu with Anthony, but this house has meaning for her. The sadness in her eyes tells me how painful the loss will be.

"No, you don't understand. I told the press some stuff about my dad. Bobby and I were out, and someone knifed his tire. I was furious with my dad for trying to ruin the one good thing I had going for me. I called a friend who works at a rag mag and dished out a bunch on my dad. This is the punishment. I swear I will repay you for everything, Emma." The tears flow freely from my eyes. Guilt overwhelms me. I look up to see Emma shaking her head.

"We're insured. It looks like a total loss to the interior. I'll call the insurance company in the morning. Don't worry, Roxy; everything in here is replaceable. As long as we're all okay, then this stuff doesn't matter." Emma leaves Bobby and me and walks out of the room.

In big black letters, the words "Emerge from your darkness" are etched on the wall's white background in my room while scraps of fabric litter the floor. It had to take hours to destroy these clothes. It looks like baskets of my clothes were dumped into a shredder and blown into the room like insulation. Remnants of Emma's blue dress are mixed throughout the carnage. A large X was cut into the bed, and the stuffing pulled out. The contents of my overturned night-stand spilled on the floor. At my feet sits my vibrator. I pick it up and notice the latex ripped from one side. I brush the tears aside as rage fills me.

A chuckle comes from across the room.

"I'm glad you think this is funny. That's my inti-mate stuff. Some creepy asshole had his hands on it. A girl has needs, and no girl I know wants some stranger's hands on her sex toys."

I'm so pissed at the thought of someone de-stroying my vibrator. I don't give a shit about the vi-brator itself; it's the fact someone held it. It's the most intimate thing in my room, and someone has had their hands on it. It's like a stranger has touched my vagina in a roundabout way. I feel dirty and violated.

"You won't need your friend, Firefly. I promise to take care of those needs." He takes the shredded phallus from my hand and tosses it into a nearby trash can.

Furious he could make light of my loss, I lash out. "I'm wallowing in the shreds of my life, and all you can do is tease me about my needs? And why in the hell do you keep calling me Firefly?"

Adding insult to injury, Bobby laughs. "You should see how you light up the room when you're mad. You glow like a firefly. As for your needs, I'm not teasing—I'm promising. We have a lot of time to make up for, and it begins tonight. Pack up what you can salvage. I'll be waiting in the living room."

Wow, was that my Bobby? *My Bobby?* Where has he been hiding? Not wanting to test his patience, I rummage through the room to find one intact pair of underwear. I look at the thong and figure it escaped because of its size. The rest of my stuff is unsalvageable. I glimpse my revered football in the corner, reduced to shreds. My hand flies to my mouth. I cannot replace things like that. *Why? Why do this?*

With the thin strip of pink fabric hanging over my finger and a candle in my hand, I walk into the living room. There are so many emotions I should feel right now. Anger... anguish... agitation... but all I can muster is the energy to feel amazement. Bobby has walked through Armageddon with me tonight and hasn't run. He has somehow taken charge, and I can't help feeling safer and perhaps even turned on.

"This is the only thing to come out unscathed." I twirl the pink panties around my index finger. "The underwear and this candle." I hold up the candle that was supposed to offer a romantic glow to the evening.

Bobby takes the panties and slips them into his

pocket. He sniffs the candle and smiles before placing it on the floor by the wall.

I'd selected a lavender-scented candle for its relaxing qualities.

He digs in his front pocket for something. "Not true. If you're hungry, I found this." He pulls out an unshelled pistachio nut.

My world spins. I stumble back and lean against the wall. "It's me. This is definitely about me." I swat the shell out of his hand. It flies across the floor and skids to a halt in front of the door. I don't want him coming into contact with my evil. In his line of work, he's touched by evil every day. It's a wonder how he stays in touch with his goodness. I refuse to let the evil that follows me taint him.

"What? Listen, we don't know for sure. Emma has an excellent argument. This could be about her. Why the freak out over the pistachio nut? I only picked it up because it seemed out of place."

"The day your car tire was slashed, I went to sit on the curb, and it was littered with shells—white shells."

The night I stepped off the bus and found my feet crunching on gravel, I could've sworn I saw someone in the shadows. Without notice, I bolt out the front door and run across the street. I scan the area, but the night is dark, and I can't see a thing.

"What are you looking for?" He hovers over me, examining the same area.

"Do you have a flashlight? You know, like one of those penlights?" He rummages through his pocket for his keys. In a second, he shines a light to reveal pistachio shells littering the ground near the big oak tree.

CHAPTER TWELVE

"Let's go." His clipped voice cuts through the air as he helps me up and tucks me protectively to his side. Quickly, he walks me to the car and opens the door for me to enter. "Stay here with the doors locked." He doesn't wait for an answer, but it's obvious he expects compliance.

On the floor by my feet is the bottle of wine we bought for our special night. Some special night... if I could gnaw out the cork, I'd have the bottle half-finished by the time he returned.

I shuffle through the mental pictures of my house and shudder. I can't imagine my father going this far. Holy shit... I was right, and someone's been following me, lurking in dark corners.

The click of the lock shakes me from the mental

image of destruction. He slides into the car and turns to look at me.

"We are going to meet with your dad tomorrow. I'll call in the morning to make an appointment. Don't worry. We will sort this out. In the meantime, you need to take a few days off work."

"I can't take off work. I have commitments, rent to pay." My hackles rise as I listen to him dictate to me.

"You're not safe at home; what makes you think you'd be safe at work? What kind of man would I be if I didn't protect you? You're important to me."

He slides his palm down my cheek. The gesture would usually comfort me, but given the situation, I refuse to be handled. I pull his hand away from me and turn to face forward.

"Don't tell me what to do. I've had enough of that all my life." I cross my arms in front of my body and stare out the window.

"I thought you'd argue about seeing your dad. I didn't expect such a powerful reaction to taking time off work."

He turns the key, and the engine roars to life. It sounds angry and loud, and the throaty growl almost mimics the ire I feel.

"I'm not taking time off work."

"Can you humor me for a day or two? Emma will not charge you rent when you can't live there. I'm not charging you to live with me, and you will be living with me." It's a statement of fact, not a request, and his assumption infuriates me.

"Do you think you can bully your way around because I'm vulnerable? I won't have you controlling me, too." I turn my head toward the window again and watch as Anthony and Emma exit the house. It's funny to see them lock the door when there's nothing left to protect.

"No, but at this moment, I'm in a better frame of mind to make good decisions. This is what I do, Roxy. Let me do it for you—let me help solve this thing."

There is such sincerity in his voice that my anger ebbs. Maybe I misinterpreted his demands. He just wants to care for me, and it's been so long since I had someone who did. The feeling is unfamiliar because I've been doing everything for myself for so long, and I have a hard time letting go.

Everything has become so muddy. My steely resolve is in danger of collapse, and I want to melt against him and let him help shoulder the burden. His hand reaches up to cup my face, and it's over. I belong to him—my heart already knows it, but my head is slowly catching up.

"All right, Fletch, let's solve this thing."

"Fletch?" He cocks his head in question.

"I can't call you 'lover boy' in public. Since you dubbed me Firefly, it's only right you get a nickname, too. You're my male version of Jessica Fletcher, so I think Fletch is fitting."

"I'd like to think I'm more attractive than her, but if you're into an aging woman with silver hair, who am I to judge? However, if your tastes lie in that direction, our relationship will go very differently than I'd planned." He chuckles, then leans over and kisses my forehead. "Let's go home."

Home.

We travel the distance in silence as my thoughts race between what happened to my home and what may happen to my body. I vacillate between anger and excitement. The rush of emotions makes everything more intense. By the time we arrive at his apartment, my body sizzles with tension.

"I'd ask you to help me with my bags, but..." I pick up the bottle of wine from the floor and hold it in front of me. "I can handle this on my own."

He pulls my pink string of underwear from his pocket. "I've got your clothes."

We both look at the scrap of fabric in his hand and laugh. I have to find the humor in the situation, or the entire event will undo me. I make a mental note to call Emma tomorrow. She'll blame herself, and I want to set the record straight. This situation was not aimed at Emma; it was targeted at me—I was the intended mark. The perpetrator hit a bulls-eye dead center; the spot most vulnerable—my home.

We enter through the security door and take the elevator to the third floor. He opens the door and guides me into his apartment. His cologne hangs in the air and folds around my senses like a terry bathrobe, and it warms me but prickles my skin.

He takes the bottle of wine from my hand and walks to the kitchen—the apartment is tidy. He rummages through the cabinets, the clinking sound signals he's found the wineglasses. The thump of the cork as it leaves the bottle makes my mouth water. I need the numbing effect of alcohol.

He walks into the living room and places the two glasses of wine on the coffee table. I stand in the center of the room, taking in the calm serenity of his apartment. His place is like the Ritz compared to the rat hole mine is now. It's crazy how a few hours can change everything. The dichotomy between our homes is mind boggling. His is neat, whereas mine's a war zone.

"Come sit with me. It's been a stressful night. Let's try to relax for a few minutes." He sits on the sofa and pats the cushion next to him. I look at it, then at his lap. Instead of sitting next to him, I toss my jacket aside and crawl into his lap. I need to be in his arms where everything is all right.

"I have nothing left."

The realization finally hits me. I have the clothes on my back, a stuffed monkey, and a pink pair of panties—that's it. I couldn't go to work if I wanted to because I have nothing to wear. The enormity of the situation settles in and chills me to the bone: The scribed words of hate throughout the house, the destruction of everything, the shells left as a calling card. It's all too much, and my body shakes. Whether it's fear, cold, or shock, I have no idea. Silent tears fall down my cheeks, his lips press against my hair, the simple gesture ungluing me. Sobs rack my body.

"Shh," he whispers against my hair. "I've got you. Everything will be okay. You're not alone." His warm arms tighten around my body like a chrysalis, a protective cocoon. I curl into his lap with my head on his chest. Despite the imperfect circumstances, this is a perfect moment.

"I think I could love you, Bobby." My vulnerability has stolen my filter.

"I think I could get used to that, Roxy." He tilts my head and takes my lips in a gentle kiss. The emotions behind it are so powerful, my heart stills.

The tension in him lessens as we hold each other in beautiful silence. Although his anger is always in check, it was present at the house. I saw it the minute he walked out. His training hides his fury, but I saw it because deep down, I know him. It hits like a tidal wave. A ripple of reaction flows from my head to my toes. Even after all these years, we never lost our connection.

"Are you cold?" His hands skim over my raised skin.

"I don't know what I am. One minute I'm freezing, the next, I'm filled with so much rage I fear I might combust. We almost stayed at my place. We could've been caught in the middle of that madness."

"The thought has occurred to me, but we weren't. We're okay. You're tensing up again, so let's get you relaxed. A hot bath will help." He slides from the couch and leaves me to rest. Exhausted from the emotional hits of the day, I doze.

The cushion dips, waking me from my dreamless slumber. "Hey, I ran you a bubble bath." Strong arms slide under my body and lift me into his arms. Steam rises from the bubble-filled bath, fogging the mirrors. The candle's soft light casts a glow across the water, making it appear as if thousands of diamonds float on the surface. Set gently on my feet, he undresses me. Piece by piece, he discarded my clothes until I stand naked in front of him. His eyes sweep my body appreciatively. Although I'm confident, this moment isn't intended to seduce, the firelight dancing off his face sends heat to my belly.

I step into the hot water and slide my tired limbs into the foam. "Join me."

The words come from the neediest part of me. Tonight is not the time to be alone. Within seconds, he's gloriously naked and sliding into the bath behind me. Cradled between his legs, I relax against his chest.

"Hmm," I purr. His arms slip down me. With fingers intertwined, we lean back and soak away the tension of the day.

"Is your dad capable of what we saw tonight?"

"I'm not sure. It's never been this serious, but if he didn't orchestrate it, then someone else did."

My mind presses its memories to flesh out any clues, but I come up blank. There's nothing to gain by destroying my home. It didn't remove me from Bobby; it sent me into his arms, house, and bed.

"Please take a few days off. I'd feel more comfortable if you did."

He's aware of my need to feel in control; it must have taken a lot for him to ask. Earlier, he was demanding, but now, I've softened his resolve.

"I have tomorrow off. I'll call out Thursday, but I'll need to work on the weekend. It's busy, and they'll need me, but I'll be safe."

"I'll drive you when I can, and I'll pick you up nightly." His voice sounds resigned. He's not happy, but he's not fighting it. "I understand your decision to go back to work. It's important to get back to your normal routine after a traumatic event. But I hope you understand my reluctance to let you go—your safety is important to me."

"I get it. I'll take the ride." Other than the fact

that I don't know the bus route from Bobby's place to Trax, the idea of being taken and collected calms me considerably.

He soaps up his hands and rubs my body. One hand cups my breast while the other slides over my stomach, then between my legs. Without modesty, they fall open. His feet wrap around my ankles and pull. The action spreads my legs wide. Human stirrups hold me open for him.

"Is this okay?"

Why in the hell is he asking? I want to feel, not think.

"Mmm, hmm."

His fingers slide through my pleated flesh. Even in the water, I can feel my slickness build. His fingers slide across the swollen nub as I labor for breath.

"Feel good?" His voice is wavering.

"Oh, God."

"Nope, it's me, Rox."

His hardness swells against my back, and his fingers stroke my heat. Pinned, I can barely move, but I lift my hips to reach him. With wanton abandon, I moan. Turning my head, I stretch my neck to steal a kiss. With my lips turn skyward, his mouth captures mine. His tongue slides into my mouth just as his fingers slide into my body. I buck, and water spills over the tub. Rolling my nipple with the fingers of one hand, exploring me with the other hand, he stimulates every erogenous zone I have. Bound with his fingers inside me, his tongue in my mouth, and his thumb stroking my nipple, I reach the sweetest release of my life. My body stills as the waves of pleasure wash over me. He pulls the last shudder from me before he removes his fingers from my entrance.

Feeling loose, I relax against him. I came entirely apart in his hands and now feel euphoric—bliss. I try to turn and reciprocate the act.

"No."

"What do you mean, no? You're always telling me no." I struggle to break free of his human ankle cuffs.

"Roxy, I wanted you to relax. Let me give you something without taking anything."

Where did this man come from?

"I want to give." I'm not a selfish lover. Sex is give and take. Hopefully, I can give more than I take.

"Not tonight. Don't think for a minute I got nothing out of that. It was damn sexy. Your body responded to me. I made you come with my touch, and you shattered in my hands."

Laughter gurgles from my chest. "Yes, I did. Hell, I can just about come from your gaze."

He shifts in the tub with his chest expanding against my back. If I can't stroke his tool, then at least I can stroke his ego.

"When I said I'd give you a night to remember,

this isn't what I had in mind. We could've done without the break-in, but all in all, it's been a special night."

Did my heart just skip? "Despite everything wrong that's happened, you are the one thing that's right."

We relax in the tub until the water cools and our skin prunes.

CHAPTER THIRTEEN

Music plays softly in the distance. The Eagles? Yep, the Eagles. I lie naked in his bed and listen to him sing the lyrics to "Love Will Keep Us Alive." He's no Timothy B. Schmit, but he sounds pleasant enough. What a perfect way to wake up. My body is sated, and my heart feels full. I close my eyes and try to burn the moment into a memory.

"Hey, beautiful."

My eyes fly open at his greeting. "You scared the hell out of me. You need to make a noise or something. You're like a freaking ninja... silent and deadly. You almost gave me a heart attack."

"I didn't intend to scare you. I just came to wake you up and ask how you slept." I feel bad for snapping at him; he was just trying to be sweet. He even came bearing gifts—freshly brewed coffee scents the air. "So, how did you sleep?"

"Better than ever." If I told the truth, I sleep best when I'm next to him. I've had more peaceful nights in the last few days than in the previous several years.

"I'm glad. I can only imagine how you'll sleep tonight." A knowing smile crosses his face. A blush heats mine.

He hands me a cup of steaming coffee and slides next to me on the bed. His fingers comb through my unruly mass of hair. "I took the day off today. We have a lot to do."

Taking a sip of coffee, I nuzzle my body next to his. Although I don't have a stitch of clothing on, I feel comfortable in my nakedness.

"You took the day off? Why?"

"You've forgotten about the meeting I set up with your father? You may have also forgotten about your lack of clothes, but don't worry, I washed what you wore yesterday. I know how you have an aversion to putting on day-old underwear, and I don't blame you." His finger twirls lazily in my hair. It feels like something two people who know each other well would do. "When you get up, we'll have breakfast, and then I'll take you shopping. You can start to rebuild your wardrobe." He takes in my body from tip to toe. His laughter makes my toes curl. "Am I stupid? I could throw away your clothes and hold you hostage. Now there's an idea."

"How well do you think that would go for you? You would have to leave for work, eventually. There's nothing more dangerous than a naked woman with an attitude." I set my coffee next to the bed and hop to my feet. My fist comes in front of me in a defensive posture, and his face contorts with laughter.

"You are so cute standing there ready to fight. You have it wrong, though." He walks to my side and realigns my fists. "Never put your thumbs inside your fist. If you hit someone, you'd break it."

Naked in his room, he gives me a self-defense lesson.

"What do I do if someone grabs me from behind?" I walk my naked behind up against his clothed body.

He groans. "I'll never allow that to happen, but if someone grabbed you from behind, just keep in mind you have several limbs. Your attacker can't control all of them at once. You can stomp on a foot or throw your head back into their body. If you're lucky, you'll knock the wind out of them or maybe break a nose. Do whatever you can to gain a second, an inch, an edge. Letting the full weight of your body drop like a sack of rocks sometimes works, too."

"Like this?" I press my naked bottom tight

against him. "Wrap your arms around me." I let my weight fall, but he catches me.

"I knew what you were going to do, so it didn't catch me off guard." He tosses me on the bed and props himself beside me.

"Can we stay in bed all day? You can give me more self-defense tips." My fingers trace his lips. I would rather kiss him than talk about self-defense and parental visits.

"You are testing my resolve, Roxy. I'm hanging by a thread here. My man brain says I've got a beautiful naked woman in my bed, and I'm an idiot for not stripping down and taking her. My professional brain says we have to get this straightened out. It's killing me, but I have to let the professional brain win right now. Tonight is another story. We have an appointment with your father after lunch. He's graciously put us on his calendar for three o'clock." The mention of my father shifts the mood of the morning. What was becoming light has turned to darkness.

"Hmm." I sit up, grab my coffee from beside the bed, and savor the potent brew. It's going to take a few more cups before I'm ready to face the day. "I don't want to see my father. I'd rather stay here and go with plan A. The one that has you naked in bed with me."

Bobby growls as he leaps off the bed. "God, Roxy, stop killing me. I'm trying to do the right thing here.

We have to get our ducks in a row." His pleading eyes weaken my resolve to stay. I know he's right—to have a future, I need to visit the past.

"I can't believe he would want to see me. Does he know I'm coming with you?" I can't imagine being in the same room with him. *He's* pure evil. He always had a mean streak. It was harder to notice when I was looking at him through the lens of a child who wanted love and acceptance.

"I made that clear when I talked to him." He pulls me to my feet and directs me toward the bathroom. "I set a fresh towel in the bathroom. Use my toothbrush now, and we'll pick you up one today. I'll meet you in the kitchen when you're done showering. I'm making pancakes." He kisses me on the cheek, swats me on my butt, and heads out the door.

I put my coffee on the nightstand and trek to the bathroom. If the shit is going to hit the fan, then I want to be as clean and well presented as I can be before I enter the storm. Oh, what a shitstorm it's going to be. I step in the steaming water and let it run over my body. I squeeze a dollop of shower gel into my palm and spread it over my skin. The citrus scent brings back memories of our perfect night. Perfect, except it's not forever. It's for now. In an ideal world, this is how it would always be.

Him.

Me.

Us.

Together.

I dry myself off and find my clothes folded neatly on the dresser. Inhaling the fresh scent, I press them to my chest and hug Bobby's sweet gesture. No man has ever done my laundry. After I'm dressed, I shuffle to the kitchen, approaching breakfast with trepidation. Once breakfast is finished, we'll move toward lunch and then the three o'clock meeting.

"Blueberry syrup or maple?" He stands in front of me with two plates of pancakes. A red-checkered apron hangs loosely around his neck, which he then takes off and puts away.

"Maple all the way. Why do you have blueberry syrup? Who uses that?" My face wrinkles in distaste. The thought of berry-flavored syrup makes me shudder.

"My mother likes it. She gave it to me as a gift. I have to agree with you, it's awful, but I wanted you to have options." He takes the small bottle of syrup, squeezes a drop on the edge of his pancake, and tosses the rest in the wastebasket. "Now I can tell her I used it."

"You have a sliding scale for accuracy, don't you?" I tilt my head and wait for his reply.

"No, I have a rigid scale with hurting my mom's feelings. I refuse to do it. I can honestly say I used it, and she will be pleased. I don't have to love it."

"Mark my words, next Christmas she'll buy you a case." I pour the maple syrup on my pancakes and watch it drip over the edge.

"No, I get gift cards for Christmas, food items for Easter, books for my birthday—she's predictable. But your family isn't, so why don't you tell me about them? You have had no contact with them in years. Why is that?" With his brows furrowed, he gives me a *tell-it-to-me-straight* look. He's not settling for the bits and pieces I've been willing to feed him. He wants full disclosure.

CHAPTER FOURTEEN

"There's no mystery. My dad wrote me off. I told you this already." I don't want to keep going over this story. After today, I want it to be over. "I wouldn't date my dad's partner. He's been with the firm since the beginning. My father was willing to trade me for loyalty. I decided I wasn't something he could barter."

"How old is this guy?"

"He's in his forties, but his age isn't what's important. The point is, I didn't do his bidding, and he cut all ties with me. He couldn't make me behave, so he made me disappear." I drag my last bite of pancake through the syrup.

"How do you feel about that?"

That's an interesting question. How should I feel?

"It's hard to say. Some days I feel sad, but some days I'm angry. It would be nice to have a family, but most days, I'm okay with it. I've finally reached a place where I've accepted my life for what it is, although it's taken a while to get there." When I think of family, Chris, Trevor, Emma, Kat, and Bobby come to mind.

"You have two sisters and a mother. What mother turns her back on her daughter?" He picks up our plates and walks to the sink to rinse them off.

"A mother who likes her lifestyle more than her children. A mother who is out of it more than she's in it. As for my sisters, I imagine I persuaded them to 'give me space.'" I air-quote the three words for effect.

"Damn, but they're your sisters. My brothers could never stay away from me."

"Money is a powerful motivator, Bobby. My oldest sister, Rosanne, is married to an associate. If her husband couldn't influence her, then her compliance would be guaranteed by her love of designer clothes." I crumble up the napkin and shoot for a three-pointer. The wad of paper falls perfectly into the can. "My younger sister, Reanne, loves law school and Prada. She's a daddy's girl, so I can't imagine her rocking the boat. Every family has a black sheep. I'm the Somervilles'." Being dismissed by my family nearly destroyed me. It was years before I could think about them without crying.

"Your family isn't loyal." He twists a kitchen towel in his hands before tossing it aside. "I'm not sure I'm interested in meeting with your father today. I'm so angry at what he put you through." He approaches me from behind and wraps his arms around me. I could stay in his embrace all day.

"So, let's cancel the appointment and do something fun. We could go back to bed." The chair tips backward as I tilt my head like a human PEZ Dispenser.

Will he submit to my request?

His grim expression speaks loudly. He won't be swayed.

"Tempting, but not going to happen. It nearly killed me to leave you naked in bed this morning, but this has to be done. You need to face him and tell him to stop. It's getting out of hand. It's getting dangerous."

"I'm afraid." There it is. It's out there—the problem I've faced for years. The ugly truth—avoidance is easier than confrontation.

"I'm going to be with you every minute. You don't have to do this alone." He turns the chair and pulls me to my feet. It would be easy to slide into his arms and let him lead the way. However, isn't it time to step up and fight for what's right? Hasn't this whole week led me to this place?

Time to pull up my big girl panties.

"You're right, and I can do this." The words sound false in my ears, but I have several hours to program myself into believing them. "Shall we go? I'm ready for some retail therapy."

"Let's go. I call dibs on choosing the bras and panties." He dashes past me and grabs the keys from the hall table. He appears motivated.

"You don't even know what size I wear." I find myself pushed against the wall, with his hands cupping my breasts. Greedy palms skirt down my body to take in handfuls of my ass. Wow, Fletch uses interesting investigative tools, ones I think I love. *And he wants to go shopping?* Condoms. Condoms had better be on the list because I don't think I can go another day without having this man inside me. Judging by the bulge pressing into my stomach, I think he's on board.

"I got it now." He turns and leaves me standing in the hallway. Calling over his shoulder, he says, "I could buy a ball of twine and braid you a pair of underwear, and it would cover more than what you wore yesterday. I'm choosing the undergarments." He's either brave or stupid. What man goes shopping with a desperate woman?

"If I'd known we were going shopping, I could've

invited Chris and Trevor; there's nothing like a queer eye for a straight guy intervention."

"Call, and they can meet us for lunch."

Running to keep up with him, I grab my purse from the floor and walk out the front door. Once in the car, I pull out my phone and text my best buddies. We exchange messages and agree to meet at Ahz for lunch. Trevor insists on a private fashion show while we dine.

"We're all set. We're meeting the boys at one o'clock at Ahz. Where do you want to start?" It's a silly question for a man with lingerie on the brain.

AT THE MALL, he never leaves my side. We walk from store to store, picking up basics like jeans, T-shirts, socks, shoes, and a dress to wear to the meeting with my father. Sephora is the next stop. I look at the woman behind the counter whose name tag reads Trisha.

"Can you make me look human again, Trisha?"

The counter attendant gives me a startled look. "You're already beautiful, but I've been known to improve perfection. Have a seat." She shows me to an empty chair and works her magic. Bobby stands to the side, mesmerized by the process.

Twenty minutes later, I transform into a

Somerville—flawless makeup—lousy attitude. All I need is lipstick. Trisha hands me two options; one is red, and the other pink.

I look at the name on the cylinders. One is called Fire Down Below, the other Fetish. Deciding to put my attitude to use, I hop off the seat and walk to Bobby. On my tiptoes, I whisper in his ear. His mouth falls open, and I reach up and pluck at his lower lip.

"I'll take them both. I'll wear Fetish now and save Fire Down Below for later." I look over my shoulder and smile at Bobby. He shakes his head. Is his mind in the same place as mine? If I had a fire down below, it's because he lit it and fanned the flames.

Trisha bags my purchases and walks them to the front of the store. Next on the list—underwear.

We walk into Victoria's Secret and set our bags on the floor next to a chair. I let my body fall comfortably into the plush cushions.

"You're not done. You need bras and underwear. Get up." He reaches for my hands, but I evade his grip.

"Oh, no, you don't, mister. You insisted this was your job, so off you go. I like pink." I pull out my phone and pretend to ignore him.

He leans down, so we are face to face. "I like pink, too. Especially, lips—both kinds." He winks before he pushes away and leaves me sitting alone with a twitch between my legs.

I take the time to text Kat and Emma.

Hey Girls,

I need some stress relief. I hoped you could meet me at The Smash Shack tomorrow at four. I'm feeling the need to destroy something. We could do Chinese after—my treat.

Rox

Within seconds, Emma responds with a *yes,* followed by an exclamation point. Kat replies a minute later with *see you there.*

It's all set. Whoever came up with throwing dishes at a wall and charging for it was a genius. I can envision the words I'll write on those plates tomorrow. Dad. Mom. Creepy stalker. It's the power of destroying whatever is written that's really cathartic. It's healing to watch my fears disintegrate into shards —too bad life isn't so easy.

"Hey, I have a dressing room set up for you." Bobby pulls me to my feet and walks me into the nearby room.

"You can't be in here." I push at his chest and shove him toward the door.

"Not true. I've asked the saleswoman to keep an eye on your bags. As your shopper, I have a responsibility to make sure my selections fit properly. Strip, my lovely. You have a lot to try on." He pulls at my clothes until I stand naked in front of him.

"This is awkward, Bobby. You're looking at me like you want to devour me, and I'm supposed to act like nothing is up?" One arm crosses over my breasts while the other cups between my legs.

"I want to devour you. You're right on the mark." He hands me a pretty lace bra and underwear set. "Try this one."

I look at the cup size and give him a look that says, *How could you possibly know?*

"I cheated. I looked when I did your laundry. All is fair in love and war."

"What is this love or war?"

I slide the bra into place. I don't need to try on the underwear, as I already know they'll fit. Besides, something about trying on lingerie that someone may have already put on gives me the willies.

He looks at my lace-covered breasts and whistles. "I love that bra. It's a keeper." I try on several bras only for his benefit. I'm positive they'll fit, but his reaction to me in them is hot. A glance at the rise in his pants tells me he thinks it's hot, too. The last thing he shows me is a pair of thigh highs and a garter belt. The matching bra is a demi-cup, which is basically a shelf for my boobs.

"I'm not trying that on. There is no way I'm

wearing that anywhere." I bend over to pick up my pants—time to get dressed.

He pushes himself tight against my backside. I can feel his erection pressing against my ass cheeks.

"We're getting it. You'll wear it for me tonight with the lipstick."

"What if I don't want to?" The moisture builds between my legs—I like this game.

He slides his hand around my stomach and down to my slick, hot center.

"I think you want to."

I collapse against him as he fingers my opening. His breath whispers against my neck. "I want you now." My heart leaps in my chest.

"Wouldn't that be against the law?" I have no idea how my boggled mind came out with a clear thought. I'd let him take me now, no matter the consequences.

"Probably, but it could be worth the risk." He slides his fingers inside of me, dragging them, torturously out of me, leaving a slick trail where his fingers skimmed my body.

My moan fills the room. "I'm definitely worth the risk," I say as I grind myself more firmly against him.

A voice from the other side of the door asks, "How's everything going? Do you need me to get you a different size?"

Timing... why does everyone have such lousy timing?

We both call out "no" in unison. The swish of the saleswoman's skirt fades as she walks from the room.

"Grrr." The roar of his frustration vibrates through the small changing room. His ragged voice wafts over my trembling flesh. "Get dressed, my little spark, and meet me out front. We'll finish this tonight."

He helps me stand on my own. An adjustment to his pants occurs before he kisses me, leaving me naked and full of desire.

I wasn't sure he'd be able to walk out of the changing room yet, but the bags he'll be carrying will disguise his bulging desire.

I hear the faint sound of rustling bags as he walks away. In the distance, he whistles, "Love Will Keep Us Alive." He's a keeper. It's amazing what that man can do with his fingers.

CHAPTER FIFTEEN

We arrive at Ahz just before one o'clock. The hostess escorts Bobby and me to the booth where we find Chris and Trevor wrapped around each other.

"Get a room." I scoot into the seat and pull Bobby close. After his tease in the dressing room, I owe him big time. I slide my hand between his legs and clutch his sack.

He coughs, pulls my hand to his knee, and says, "What's up?" His eyes drift to the men sitting across from us.

Running my hand back up to cup his package, I rub back and forth, making sure he rises to the occasion. This time, he places his hand back over mine and lifts my fingers to his lips. I expect him to kiss them, but a big shock occurs when he bites firmly on my knuckles. A screech leaves my lips, but it's quickly suppressed with a kiss.

Just before he pulls away, he whispers a warning. "Behave." I am reasonably sure that is not what I want to do.

Chris begins the conversation, which is never a good idea to let him lead, as he has no filter. Trevor is more reserved, and Chris is, well, Chris. What you see is what you get. Authentic people have always been a pull for me. It's the number one issue I've had with my family. Nothing was real—they fabricated everything for the masses. *Look at the perfect Somerville family.* What a load of crap.

"So, Bobby, tell us about your pistol." Chris leans on the table and cradles his chin in his hands.

Trevor laughs.

I eye Bobby for his response.

"My service weapon is a Glock 23." He looks at me, perplexed.

"Ooh, is it big?" Chris is playing it up.

Trevor and I can barely hold it together.

"It's big enough to get the job done. Why are you so interested in my weapon?" His eyes move between the three of us at the table.

"Leave him alone," I say, coming to his rescue.

"Trevor and I are looking out for her. She loves a man in uniform. She once dated a firefighter, but he lacked in the hose department. We were—"

"Stop it. Bobby doesn't deserve this. I'm sure his pistol packs a punch. He's fully loaded and ready to shoot at a moment's notice. Now stop it." I turn to Bobby and give my best I'm-so-sorry look.

Laughter fills the table as all three men look in my direction. My face feels hot, and it has to be beet red. I'm used to the men across from me. They both have a raunchy sense of humor. In my line of work, I'm exposed to that kind of talk every day. Bobby's smile brings me relief. He doesn't look shocked in the least and actually appears to be having fun with it.

"I'm glad you're confident in my shooting ability. I'd hate to end up in a pile next to the fireman who lacks a good hose. I don't think you've told me about him."

"You all need to stop. I'm not discussing the details of my man's pistol with the public." Turning toward Bobby, I grumble, "And I'm not talking about a previous encounter with you." I pick up the menu and look over my choices.

Why did I bring him to lunch with these two men?

The server arrives in time to save me from more ribbing. We order lunch and talk about more appropriate subjects.

Trevor asks about the shopping trip and what we have planned for the rest of the day. News of the break-in has already spread, and Chris and Trevor are shocked by what they heard.

"Believe it or not, we are going to visit my father after lunch. This craziness has to stop. Emma's house was destroyed because of his nonsense."

Chris pipes in, "Emma said the break-in was aimed at her, but you think it was your dad?" He bobs his head as if bouncing both ideas across his brain.

"Yes, it was definitely my dad. Bobby found a pistachio shell in the house. Neither Emma nor I eat them. I've been finding them around lately. It's a bit scary to know someone is watching me."

"Very, but let's talk clothes." Trevor shivers. "What are you wearing to visit your father?"

"I was going to wear a dress, but I'm wearing what I have on."

Looking appalled, Trevor slams his hand on the table. "Bullshit." Chris's and Bobby's heads turn toward him.

"What do you mean, bullshit? He doesn't care what I look like." I'm lying to myself. My dad is all about appearances. Walking into his office in a T-shirt and jeans would be a stab to his image. Too bad he left me with nothing to wear. "I'm not representing the Somervilles, so I couldn't care less what he thinks."

"I don't care about the Somervilles. You're representing yourself," he looks at Bobby, "and your man. You owe it to yourself to walk into his office feeling proud. Despite his trying to crush you, you've survived." Trevor looks at Bobby. "Can you grab the nicest thing you bought today? After lunch, we'll go to my office and do clothes and hair. Your makeup looks great. What color is that lipstick because it's fabulous?"

Bobby blurts out, "Fetish. It's called Fetish. I also bought one called Fire Down Under." He's like a kid with a new toy. He's obviously looking forward to the red lipstick.

Chris chimes in, "One more color and two more sets of lips and you could have a rainbow party." A foolish grin takes up his face.

"Stop." I hold up my palm in front of Chris's face. "All three of you are awful." Looking at Bobby, I say, "Wipe that grin off your face. If you think I'm sharing my lipstick or your pistol with anyone, you're crazy." The conversation ends with the arrival of lunch.

Lunch topics cover Emma's recent nuptials and speculation about when Kat and Damon will tie the knot. The afternoon did what Bobby probably wanted it to, distracted me. He went to the car to get the bag containing the dress and sandals while Chris headed back to work.

Trevor walked us through a labyrinth to his office.

The choice for eating at Ahz was an easy decision. Trevor works in the building, and Chris only works a few blocks away. Besides that, the food is excellent, and the atmosphere is relaxing.

"Perfect."

Trevor twirls me in a circle as he looks at the pale-blue sundress he had me put on. The silver strappy sandals are a perfect choice. He reaches into his desk drawer for his straight iron and immediately plugs it in. This man is on a mission. Why is it gay men always seem to have what a girl needs?

He pulls my long strands through the hot device, leaving my hair flat against my back. He rummages through his drawer and comes out with a small flower clip.

"Whose barrette is that?" I ask as I look at the sparkling clip.

He places it strategically in my hair. "Chris's. You know how he is. He likes bling." Trevor turns me toward Bobby and gives me a nudge forward.

"Wow, you were perfect before. What are you now?" Bobby takes in a big breath and then lets out a long exhale.

"You're ready to conquer the world. You go, girl, and don't take any shit from your father. Chris and I will expect a full report on Friday at Trax."

At the mention of Friday, I glance at Bobby. He

shows no reaction to the idea of me working. I smile. Maybe Fletch didn't have perfect recall.

I thank Trevor for his help, and we make our way to the garage. He leans against the car, pulls me into his arms, and settles a soft kiss on my lips.

"Roxy, you look stunning. You look like you did on graduation day. You were dressed in a little purple dress and heels. Your hair was almost exactly like it is now, only it was shorter then."

"How do you remember what I wore? That was years ago. I barely remember what I wore yesterday."

"You were naked in my bed yesterday." His eyes light up at the mention of me being nude. But then as if he just realized something, his face turns serious. "I thought we had an understanding, and you would be taking a few days off. You're not working Friday." He requires unquestioning obedience.

So, he has perfect recall. "I have to work. We'll talk about it later. I'm not fighting with you right before I fight with my dad." I try to distract him with a deep kiss, and it works for a moment. Then, breaking free, he turns around and helps me into the car.

Once in the car, he directs the conversation back to work. "Roxy, until we figure out who's following you, you shouldn't be left alone. What if someone grabbed you? I couldn't live with myself if something happened to you. Humor me and let me keep you safe."

"I understand you care. It warms my heart. But you have to understand I've been dealing with this for years. If someone were going to hurt me, wouldn't they have already done it? I won't hide in fear. I have a life, and I plan to live it. Avoiding something will not make it go away. I'll be careful."

"This conversation isn't over; it's just over for now." He starts the engine and sets out for my father's office.

It's been a long time since I've been there. Somerville and Sloan take up a half-block of prime Los Angeles real estate that houses everything from criminal attorneys to ambulance chasers. My dad has his fingers in all the pies. Bobby finds a car pulling out and slides into the space. Parking downtown is always a nightmare. He runs around and opens the door for me. Dressed in khaki pants and a navy-blue polo shirt, he could've just come off the golf course.

He fits in.

I never did.

I'm glad he's here—his presence brings me strength. He takes my hand and helps me out of the car. With my quaking knees, I wobble on my heels. The door closes behind me, and the beep of the lock ends any notion that I can climb back inside the car and hide.

"Are you okay?" His voice filled with concern. He pulls me against him and flattens us both against the building. "Look at me." He pulls my chin up, so I am looking into his eyes. "He has no control over you. You are here to tell him to stop terrorizing you. You are not here for his approval. Do you understand?"

"Yes," I say in a wavering voice. "The awful truth is I want his approval. I've wanted it my entire life and never got it." Admitting this is like digging up an old skeleton. It's scary at first, but in the end, it's only bones. Figuring out what to do with the information is the dilemma. Do I bury the bones and let them haunt me forever, or do I accept them for what they are, remnants of my past? I've never vocalized my needs to anyone before, but I keep doing it with Bobby.

"I'm aware of how important it is to have your parents be proud of you. Your father may disagree with you, but I bet he's proud you've been able to make it in life without his influence. If he's not, he's an asshole." On that note, he pulls me into the front door and walks to the main reception desk. "Detective Anderson and Ms. Somerville to see Trenton Somerville."

The guard at the desk eyes Bobby first. He glances at me before sending us up to the twenty-fourth floor. The elevator rises quickly, with no stops in between. The doors open to a beautifully decorated waiting area.

Business must be good.

Before we approach the desk, Bobby cups my head between his palms and looks straight into my eyes.

"Show him who you are. Lift your perky nose and pull back those shoulders. Ignite your ember, Firefly. You got this." He grazes my lips with his, lowers his hand to lock it with mine, and purposefully walks me to the enormous desk in the center of the room.

"Can I help you?" the sour-faced secretary asks. Her gaunt face is pinched like a puckered anus. She must be new because his last secretary was younger and possessed a personality. By the monotone of this woman's voice, it's clear she has nothing but a nasty demeanor.

"I'm Roxanne Somerville, and I'm here to see my father."

CHAPTER SIXTEEN

We're ushered through the large, imposing doors.

My father sits in the power position at his desk. With a nod of his head, he points to the chairs in front and goes back to whatever work he is doing. I sit defiantly, and Bobby sits next to me. I shade my eyes from the harsh lighting—lighting more suited for an interrogation than a consultation. Like an ant under a magnifying glass, I sit, trapped, waiting for his words —words that have the power to burn my soul.

Silence fills the air. It's part of the plan. Ignore. Initiate. Ignite. Injure. It's how things are done. Control, it's always about power. Isn't it time I took it back?

I rise from the chair. I don't have to play by his rules because I'm a grown woman. I stand on taffy legs and totter across the room. The shuffle of papers and a clearing of a throat fill the silence. My father's voice echoes uncomfortably in my ears.

"Detective Anderson, are you here on personal or private business? When you called this morning, I thought something was amiss with my daughter, Roxanne." I turn around at the mention of my name. My father glares at me, then turns his head and continues to talk to Bobby. "She looks alive and well. What brings you here?" I inspect the man who helped bring me into the world. His only contribution was sperm and a bankroll.

"Mr. Somerville, I'm here for both personal and professional reasons. However, you should direct your conversation to Roxy, not me." My dad's eyes narrow, and his lips stretch as tight as a pair of spanks. All eyes go to me.

"Roxanne, I'm a very busy man. What do you want that requires you to bring a detective to my doorstep? It's been four years. Why visit now? Are you homeless—broke?"

He looks older than I remember. The crinkles near his eyes speak to long nights and lots of alcohol. I used to quake in his presence, but it has become clear it was never the man I feared; it was his resources. Without them, he's nothing. I squash my initial angst.

He has no hold on me anymore.

My life as Trenton Somerville's daughter was just a prologue. A brief glimpse of what was, not what has to be. Shame on him for trying to be the main character in my story. Shame on me for letting it happen for so long.

Agitation builds inside me. "Yes, I'm homeless, but that is something you already know." Here sits a man whose only joy is working. His successes are built on someone else's failures—his worth based on the crushed souls of those he conquered. I walk up to the desk and lean forward fearlessly toward him. "Last night, you went too far. I rent a room in that house. I don't own it. Why did you have your people destroy it? I came to ask you to stop." I'm now within a few inches of his face and raise my voice. "No, I came to *demand* you to stop. I'll never submit to you, so stop trying to make me." My father's face snaps back from the verbal spanking I deliver.

I look toward Bobby; his expression is unreadable. His eyes are on my father. He's in detective mode. I can see the cogs of his brain turning, and everything about him screams Jessica Fletcher. He is hard at work.

His words, *You got this,* echo through my mind. Yep, he's right. Confidence surges through me while fear evaporates like water under the desert sun.

"I have done no such thing. I haven't had you followed since the first year." Indignation ignites his face. His cheeks become the color of cherry Kool-Aid.

"That's bullshit." I push off the desk and walk to the window. I press my head against the glass, the coolness reminding me to keep my temper in check.

"Watch your mouth, young lady." My father pushes away from the desk and stands.

Bobby calmly says, "I'd recommend you keep your seat, Mr. Somerville." He doesn't raise his voice, and he doesn't change his inflection. He doesn't have to because Bobby talked with dead-serious intent.

I turn from the window to watch the exchange. Clearly, my father doesn't want to find out what Bobby might do. He sits back down obediently and grumbles.

"Years ago, you tried to force me into a relationship with your partner. You manipulated my life to your advantage. You withheld, watched, and waited. I've been evicted, fired, libeled, and attacked. If you're telling me you had nothing to do with last night's vandalism, you're a liar."

My father rises from his seat, but a glance at the stoic detective changes his mind.

"I took things from you the first year. When it was obvious you wouldn't comply with my wishes, I dismissed you. I don't have time to deal with the emotional outbursts of a child. Look around you. This is what it's all about." His eyes skim the superficial surroundings. Hard lines. Cool colors. Nothing soft and warm. This is where his world begins and ends.

His words could've eviscerated me; however, with my dad, I bled out long ago. Seeing him today just confirmed what I've always known. He has no attachment to anything but the firm.

"I have a hard time believing what I told the re-porter didn't influence you to retaliate."

"Are you talking about your little hissy fit? Is that why you did it? Did you want attention from your daddy? It's so tough being a poor-little-rich-girl." He rolls his eyes as the sarcasm drips from his thin, frigid lips. "I saw the story. At least it was accurate. You're not a liar. I wanted you to marry Todd. He was older, wiser, and I thought he could control you. You were always a pain in the ass, Roxanne, classic middle-child syndrome." For the first time in a long time, his statement makes something clear. He wanted Todd to control me, and since he controlled Todd, then in essence, he would control me.

Taking a deep breath, I hurl a few facts in his di-rection. "First, I don't want you to get yourself con-fused about being my daddy. Daddy implies sacrifice and commitment, compassion, understanding, val-ues, and relationship. You're... you're in the loosest term a father. You donated DNA and financial support."

"What did you want from me?"

Could a smart man be so dense?

"I wanted a life of my choosing. I wanted to do something other than law. I wanted to experience love. I wanted to belong to a family who cared for me." I pace the room, restless and discontent. "How are your ideal daughters—my sisters?" It's not their fault he tolerates them. They've always been pliable pleasers.

"Why ask now? You haven't contacted them for years." Smugness settles over his face like a five o'clock shadow.

"Oh, no you don't. You will not turn this around and make it my problem. I called for a year straight. I begged my sisters to meet me somewhere, anywhere. This is all on you, your need for absolute control."

"I lifted the ban after a year, and you never came around. Your mother sent you a Christmas card every year, but it came back undeliverable. She was heartbroken."

Oh, here it goes. When intimidation doesn't work, go for guilt.

"How is my mother? Is she out of rehab?" Every year, like clockwork, she enters a treatment program at the end of summer. She appears to use it as her summer camp.

"Don't be disrespectful, Roxanne; your mother has emotional problems. She's currently in Paris with Reanne. They're buying her wedding dress. She's marrying Todd Sloan this fall." The look of victory shines from his face. The information doesn't surprise me. My sisters, although we share the same DNA, are cut from a different cloth.

"Mother's only problem was marrying you. Drinking is a coping mechanism. She drinks to forget." Her life at Betty Ford probably at least resembles some kind of normal life—one she can live with.

"This conversation is getting tiresome, Roxanne. What is it you want from me? Money?" He'd never consider I might need acceptance, affection, or love. No, his mind goes to money.

Bobby rises from his seat and comes to stand next to me. "Do you have anything left to say to your father?"

"Nope, I've said it all."

"Do you mind if I have a few words with him?" He winks at me and half smiles. I turn and walk toward the door. Rather than open it and exit, I stop, wait, and listen.

"Mr. Somerville, first off, you're an idiot. You don't deserve your daughter. She's turned out to be the most amazing woman, despite you and your crazy-ass family. You'll never have to love her because my love will overwhelm her. I'll care for and protect her like you never have. I only hope you haven't damaged her ability to love. You're a failure as a father and a man." Bobby leans over the desk, taking the position of power. His six-foot-plus height towers over the small, spindly man hiding behind the enormous desk. "With you being a lawyer and all, I shouldn't have to tell you how your daughter could press charges. Stalking and filing false accusations to get her evicted is a criminal offense. It's slander, Mr. Somerville. I'm sure you're familiar with the term. I can't help but notice all these problems began when you hired someone to follow your daughter. I'll need the name of the person or company you hired for surveillance. I will not hesitate to use all the resources available to gain access to that information. Your daughter is in danger. You should be concerned, if not for her, then for the shitstorm of publicity I'll send your way should anything happen to her."

I whirl around and exit. The smile on my face is so big, it hurts. Behind me, Bobby mumbles a few choice expletives. He appears at my side. His expression is tranquil, but his body rigid.

"Shall we go?"

Despite everything, I feel free. I should be angry. Angry at myself for caring about a family not worthy of my time. Angry for wasting so much energy on meaningless people. Relief washes over me at the realization that my family is a plague and I'm immune.

"Roxanne." My father's voice soils my skin. Just being in his presence makes me want a shower. I raise my eyes in question. "Despite what you think, I love you. It's just I don't understand you. You are a Somerville, and I expect you to behave in a certain way. While I applaud your spirit, I despise your impertinence. I didn't come out here to argue. Your grandparents set up a trust for you. You reached the distribution age at twenty-one, but since no one knew where to find you, it's been collecting interest. Leave your contact information with Joan, and I will forward it to your grandparents' lawyers. Stay safe, Roxanne."

He turns and shuts the door, but it doesn't surprise me he got the last word. It's his usual practice. Did he say a trust in my name? It's not as if I couldn't be found. He didn't care enough to put forth the effort.

What an asshole.

Bobby removes his business card from his wallet, writes his contact information on the back, and sets it in front of the prune-faced woman. "Let's go. We have more important things to do."

My skin tingles under the gentle caress of his fingertips. With his hand on my back, he escorts me to the elevator. As soon as the door closes, I turn and pin him to the wall.

"That was so freaking sexy. I drenched my new panties when you threatened him." My hands run up his chest. My head settles on his breast pocket.

"Wet panties, huh? I can help with that." Inquisitive hands journey down my body to cup my bottom. "Let's go home and make love."

"Ooh, that sounds perfect. I want you inside me now." The bluntness of my words surprises me. Tact isn't my strength, but lewdness hasn't been a character flaw either.

His eyes burn with desire. Large hands glide up my body to cup my cheeks. A soft expression settles across his face. Reverence. Want. So many emotions reflect in his eyes. Silence fills the air. It's the pregnant pause before something significant happens.

"I freaking love you."

His words shock me into silence. He just said he loved me. Is it possible to love someone in so little time? We spent every day together the first two years of high school, but it's been so long since then. Is this love? I did just tell him I could fall in love with him.

The elevator doors open into the busy lobby. As people bustle about, the slow-motion sound of his voice echoes in my head. *I freaking love you.* I wrap my head around his words and declare to myself; *I freaking love that idea.*

CHAPTER SEVENTEEN

The minute we walk through the door, he strips me of my wet panties. He has me completely naked by the time we get to the bedroom. He playfully tosses me on top of the comforter, and I'm on display like a Christmas goose.

Stripping himself, he climbs up my eager body. His fingertips graze over the swell of my breasts, and I involuntarily lift to meet his touch. Torturously, slowly—too slowly—he circles the pad of his thumb near the puckered flesh of my taut nipple.

"Bobby." Little moans of pleasure add to the excitement. His attention moves to my other breast. He never actually touches my nipple; he just comes close enough to torment me.

"Please."

"Hmm." His hand cups my right breast, stealing a shudder from my tense body. In no hurry, his fingers travel to my core. "You're wet—wet for me." His words sound full of wonderment.

I'm ready for the invasion when his fingers slide along my slick center. He slips in and out, stretching me to accommodate him. My hips rise at the delicious intrusion. Hot. He makes me hot, and panting, and begging for more.

"Please."

"Please? Yes, you do please me." He pulls his fingers from inside me, leaving me empty—wanting.

"Please," I plead.

"Yes, it's my pleasure to please you." His fingers trail across my sensitive flesh. My body quivers under his touch.

"Please," I beg louder, my voice rising with my passion. My hands grasp at his body, and I grab his arm and pull him up toward my entrance.

Is this moment finally happening?

His lips seek mine, and his desperation to have me is obvious. As he deepens the kiss, the heat of his tongue scorches my senses. I shift against him, feeling his hardness poke at my thigh. Switching positions, I straddle his legs, and we seem to volley for control.

His erection sits between my thighs, and there's nothing but air between us. My hands explore his chest while his muscles ripple beneath my fingertips.

I sink my fingers into his thick brown hair and pull him closer. Close enough to taste the honeyed sweetness of his lips. The smooth stroke of his tongue builds up the heat inside me. I'm ready for him to take me.

I pull my lips from his. "I need you, Bobby. I want you." My hands drop from his head to his hardness. His breath quickens as his eyes scan my body and then settle on my chest. Passionate fire lights his face.

"I'm here."

His eyes grow wide as my taut nipples rise before him. He raises his head and burns my puckered flesh with his breath. The hot air sizzles to the apex of my thighs.

Another shift and I find myself beneath him once again. He pulls back and looks at me. It's like he's Rembrandt looking at his masterpiece. I watch him glance over me like a cherished canvas. He takes in the pigment of my skin, every nuance of my body. The distance between us allows the chill of the cool air to brush between my bare legs.

The mattress shifts under his weight. I wrap my legs around his waist and my arms around his neck. There's no way I'm letting him go now. Energy flows through my body as the prickly hairs of his legs rub against my sensitive skin. He scales me like a trained athlete climbing a revered mountain. Every touch electrifies me—tingling from the inside out, I vibrate with desire. Every kiss, every stroke, and every whisper move through me like a live current, waiting for him to release the power of it, as only he can.

"You're beautiful, Roxy. Simply beautiful."

"Hmm." My hum fills the silence.

His fingers glide over my heated skin. The soft pad of his thumb brushes over my hardened nipple. Rolling it between his fingers elicits a ragged, throaty response. He labors over my breasts. Plucking. Pulling. Pinching. Every tug on the hard buds makes me pant with need. He cups them as if sizing and weighing them. The smile on his face says they're perfect. I'm dying to feel his mouth on them. A shift of his body and my prayers are answered. Hot moisture encapsulates the tip—a pulsing sensation races to my wet center. I need more. I need everything.

He straddles my body. "You're glowing, and I knew you would. Passion ignites you." His mouth hovers over me. When his head rises, losing his heat makes me shudder.

"Bobby. Please."

The desperation in my voice has hit a nerve with him. Sliding down, he hovers above my dripping sex. I lie exposed to him. Despite trying to bring myself into a sitting position, he presses me back against the mattress. He runs his hands from my shoulders to my hips.

A gasp escapes my mouth as his fingers trace from my hip to my sex and slide up my wet slit to settle firmly on my bundle of nerves.

"I want this—all of this. I want to taste you, to be inside you. Tonight, we forget everything but us."

His words make me shake with need. The sensuality radiating from them floods me with desire. My heart pounds out a rhythm that pulses between my legs.

Raising my hips, I offer myself to him. A sly smile breaks as his tongue darts out to lick his lips. He kisses his way down my stomach until he presses his lips to the soft flesh between my legs. With a moan, I let them fall open, giving him unfettered access to my most intimate parts. Separating the folds, he explores me thoroughly. His stiffened tongue has my hips rising to meet his thrusts. A deep, ragged groan flows freely from my mouth. The sensitive nub beneath his fingers responds to his strokes. My breath hitches as he sucks the hard nub into his fiery mouth. I cry out as the feeling escalates.

"Not yet." He slows the pace and brings me down with gentle strokes. He fires me up again with the insertion of a finger. The in and out motion stokes my flame.

"Don't make me beg." I twist under his touch.

"I'd like to hear you beg." He dips his head and feasts on me again. This time, his intent is obvious.

His tongue is relentless. His fingers fill me. His lips close over me. He suckles gently at first, but with every stroke of his buried fingers, the pressure intensifies. The tingling starts in my toes.

Like mercury rising, the sensation travels up my body. Knees shaking. Breath halting. Sex pulsing. And then the orgasm rocks loose. His name flows from my lips, and the aftershocks course through my quaking limbs. He sucks and pulls until I squirm under his mouth from the intensity of his touch.

"Amazing."

He climbs up me and swipes the glistening juices from his lips as he crushes his mouth into mine. It's less of a kiss and more of a branding. Pulling away, he reminds me to breathe.

For a moment, that's all I can do.

"Bobby," I say, panting. "I want you."

I reach for his hips. Every muscle of my body feels like jelly, and my arms fall limply to my side.

"My poor girl, you're exhausted."

"I'm not too tired to make love to you." My statement is sincere. He sucked and pulled the last bit of energy I had from my body. But I'm confident I can rally if properly motivated.

"I'm ready to give myself to you." *More than ready*. I try to pull him into me. He chuckles at my impatience. With little effort, he picks me up and slides my body under the comforter. Leaning over, he kisses me. "I'll be right back."

I let out a frustrated groan. His laughter rings in my ears as I watch the firm globes of his ass disappear. I feel sated, but my heart needs a deeper connection. Every fiber of my being wants to belong to him.

He returns to his room with two glasses of wine and climbs onto the bed next to me. Pulling me into a sitting position tucked up next to his side, he is glorious in his nakedness. He sits comfortably beside me and hands me a glass of wine.

"Why won't you make love to me? I need to feel connected to you."

He did incredible things, but I feel selfish letting him give me so much without taking anything for himself. Something about not connecting our bodies makes the act less than it could be.

"I will make love to you. I want to make sure I meet your needs first. I want you to feel like the most important part of my life. If sacrificing my needs will help you understand how important you are to me, then I'll do it repeatedly." His fingers run the length of my bare arm. Bumps prickle my skin as the electrifying sensation washes over me. He's crazy if he thinks I'm not having all of him tonight.

"Bobby, you need to listen to me carefully. I've been dreaming about making love to you since the ninth grade. I'm naked in your bed. My body thrums with a desire for you. My heart aches to be close to you. Are you going to deny me the pleasure of having you?"

Silence fills the air.

"Well, put that way, no. I'll never deny you what I can easily give you."

He takes the half-full glass of wine from my hand and places it with his on the nightstand. Throwing off the cover, he exposes me for his viewing pleasure. The cool air bites at my nipples, making them stand erect. His fiery gaze heats me as his eyes devour me.

Shifting our bodies, I straddle him, sliding my legs on each side of him and pressing my chest to his face. Without a doubt, he's a boob man. He's always had a thing for my breasts. I push my cleavage into his face and sit my naked center directly over his erection. He shifts below me, and our bare parts pleasurably rub together. I'm not sure I'll ever get enough of him. Pulling away, my nipple pops from his mouth. His groan of displeasure makes me smile. All is fair in love and war. I slide down his body and come in direct contact with his beautiful erection. Thick and long, it strains against itself. My palms brush down his thighs. A hiss escapes his lips and spurs me on. I wrap my moist lips around the crown of his length, and his body stiffens as my soft tongue caresses the sensitive top.

"Oh, holy hell." His hands twine in my hair.

I slide along his shaft until my mouth is full. His gasp is my reward. The salty taste of him makes my mouth water for more. Rubbing my tongue along the underside of his hardness, I feel the large, engorged vein pulse. Up and down, I stroke him. I take him to the edge and coax him back repeatedly. His breath is labored, and his body is a mass of twitching limbs. Sitting up, I press my hands to his chest. His sleepy eyes open, and in their reflection, I see forever.

He leaps into action. In a quick move, he's back on top. We've exchanged this position several times. It's nice he can take and give. I look into his eyes, and passion darkens the centers. His pupils are large and looming and ringed by a sliver of emerald green. He lowers his body so his length slides along my crease, the heat of it searing my tissue.

His lips brush against mine, a whisper of affection breezing over my senses. "You are perfect, Roxy. You're perfect for me."

It would be easy to fall in love with him, so it's easy to let it all happen. I want to let him in—into my body—into my heart.

I feel his body stretch. I follow his motion with my eyes. He's reaching for something in the nightstand—a condom. He's always thinking, always protecting me. The tear of the wrapper breaks the silence. I inhale deeply as he rolls it over his length. A shiver of anticipation scurries up my spine. Back in position, he readies himself.

"Relax." His words lull me into a feeling of safety. His eyes lock on mine. We convey a promise that I can trust him to care for me. My hips rise. He sinks into me as I thrust my impatient hips at him. Moans fill the air as I stretch to accommodate him.

"I told you my favorite place would be right here." He moves with slow deliberation. "I love the way we fit perfectly together." His voice is like a twenty-year-old scotch—smooth and velvety.

Fire races from his words straight to my throbbing sex. His slow glide strokes my insides. Last night felt great, but today everything has changed. The L word was tossed out, and now the stakes are higher.

The look in his eyes nearly collapses my lungs, and realization strikes me. I'm the reason for his lust-filled eyes—his look of possession. This is more than sex. I can now understand his reason for waiting.

His hips rotate, and his thrusts increase in speed and power. My body responds instantly, driving hard against his arousal, and I feel like I'm floating through space tethered to him. Fire shoots through my center. Stars burst through the darkness. Light bursts behind my closed eyes. The pulsing begins in my heart and ends between my quivering legs.

I call out his name. My mind follows it with a silent

"I love you," as if *Bobby, I love you,* is his full name. I've never said those words to any man. I'm not sure I'm ready to say them now. This relationship, though new, feels comfortable, and I want to keep it that way.

He slows his pace. "Look at me, Roxy. Hearing you say my name is everything."

He continues to love me slowly, with long, lazy strokes designed to convey an emotion. Love—every stroke imparts love. I feel his body shudder above mine. The look in his eyes steals my breath away. He looks so blissfully happy. He slowly slides from my body, and we lie side by side, looking at the ceiling, sated and blissfully happy.

"Can this be love, Bobby?" Is it possible to fall in love so soon?

"Do you believe in love at first sight?"

"I never did. I didn't believe in love at all." I roll to my side and lay my head on his chest. He wraps an arm around my back and pulls me against him. "I don't have suitable role models. Love is something that happens in the movies. I serial date. I don't fall in love."

"A serial dater, huh? Is that what you thought this would be?" He chuckles.

"Yes. I thought we'd sleep together, I'd explain about my dad, and you'd run. Only, you didn't."

"Have you ever known me to run? Honestly,

Roxy, your memory sucks." His tone is disappointment mixed with humor.

"My memory sucks? What did I forget?"

"I never gave up on you. You ran, not me." He's right. I ran, not away from him, for him.

"I had to." My father had researched him. All of his information was laid out on the table when I got home. That was the intent. A silent threat that came across loud and clear. There was no way I could date the son of a bank teller.

"Damn it, Roxy. You didn't have to give me up." He pulls me onto his chest. "I was ready to fight for you." His voice is almost a whisper. "I would've fought for you."

I lift my head. His eyes are those of the boy I hurt years ago. "You fought for me today." I lay my head on his chest. "The man you turned out to be is a true match for my father." My fingers slide along his shoulder. Shoulders strong enough to bear the weight of a thousand meetings with my father. "The boy you were was not prepared for what he was capable of." No words have ever been more accurate. I regret breaking the boy's heart, but I hope to heal the heart of the man. "I'm sorry."

His lips graze the top of my head. "I loved you the moment you strutted into Spanish class wearing a short skirt and carrying pom-poms." His chest rumbles with a chuckle. "I tried out for the football team so I could watch you on the sidelines."

"I might have loved you the day you brought me your touchdown football." The ball came straight from the end zone into my hands. Sadly, it fell victim to the break-in. It was my most valuable possession and seeing it tattered in the corner was gut-wrenching.

"I loved the day you made me cookies and brought them to my house."

"I loved that you ate them despite hating walnuts." I giggle. He gagged the cookies down with a smile on his face.

"I love that you let me kiss you that day at the coffee shop."

"I loved the kiss, too. It was the day I had to say goodbye."

"Never say goodbye again, Roxy. I'll never let you go." His heart pounds loud in my ear.

"I need a new football, Fletch. That pistachio-eating bastard destroyed mine." I roll off his chest and rise to a sitting position. I lick my lips and wait for his reaction.

"No way. That was *the* football?" He rises beside me and shows his Hollywood smile.

It obviously pleases him I kept the ball all these years. "Yes, way. Call me sentimental."

"You loved me, you little liar. You loved me, and

you let me go. Who are you, Lynyrd Skynyrd?" He pegs me with a look that says, *Tell the truth*. "Was I your 'Free Bird'?"

"Don't be a nube. I was a teenage girl. Letting you go was my only option."

The day I turned my back on him changed my life. The sun was a bit duller, the air thicker. Letting go of Bobby Anderson was like letting go of a piece of my beating heart. I've been broken since then.

"I came back to you."

"I'm keeping you."

The decision was made when we made love. I knew the minute he entered me. I'd never give him up. The permanence of that thought should scare me, but it doesn't. I've never thought permanent could be part of my life or part of my vocabulary —until now.

I hold him tightly and whisper, "I could love you, Bobby Anderson."

He leans to the side and replies, "I'll make you love me, Roxy Somerville."

CHAPTER EIGHTEEN

Dressed in his T-shirt and a pair of his boxers, I walk into the kitchen to find coffee ready and a note on the table.

Roxy,

This morning I woke up the happiest man around. The air is fresher, the sun is brighter, and the future is clearer. How lucky am I to get a second chance at an epic love? You... naked... my bed! There's nothing more to say, except:

Love you,

Bobby

The man you love! (Subliminal advertising)

I pour my coffee and add the half-and-half I found in the refrigerator that I knew he got it specifically for me.

Once in the living room, I curl on the couch, re-playing yesterday's meeting in my mind. My father hasn't changed. Determined, detached, and devious are hallmarks of his personality.

That he hasn't tried to contact me after the first year gives me a stab to the heart. Most fathers would fight harder. Sadly, my father is exactly what I accused him of being, a sperm donor. Why my parents had three children is beyond me. Selfish people make awful parents. The best thing about yesterday's meeting is we both unequivocally know where the other stands.

His surly disposition didn't interfere with his ability to come across as sincere. Even Bobby didn't question his honesty. If he's telling the truth, then someone else is behind the last three years of torment. Who would spend so much time making my life miserable, and to what end? There's nothing to gain.

Burying the ugliness, I think of something pleasant. Bobby's body over mine comes to mind right away. After making love yesterday, we ordered pizza and curled up on the couch to watch *Taken*. It might not have been the best choice for the subject matter, but it was an action and adventure film, and it starred Liam Neeson. How could we go wrong? We climbed into bed and acted like sleeping together was the most natural thing to do. He made love to me again, and when we finished, I fell asleep in his arms.

I barely heard him this morning. He must have tried to be extra quiet. I woke when the bed dipped next to me. He brushed my hair from my face and kissed me goodbye, saying something about my clothes being hung in the closet and the top two drawers of his dresser being mine.

Missing him, I pick up my phone and send a text.

I miss you! Too bad we're not independently wealthy. We could stay in bed all day. :-)

His text arrives several minutes later.

I miss you too. I'd consider living like a pauper if it meant being able to spend all day with you.

I picture us living in a box on the street. I may love him, but I would hate living like that. I've down-graded enough for a lifetime. *Wow, I do love him.* It may be hard to say it out loud, but internally I know it's true.

Pauper wouldn't look good on either of us.

For all intents and purposes, I went from princess to pauper already. Once in a lifetime is enough.

We're a long way from there. I'll take care of you. Speaking of taking care of you, what do you want for dinner? I can grab something on my way home.

Shit. I forgot to tell him about my plans with Emma and Kat. I'm going to have to get used to answering to someone else. Ironically, I've spent most of my life fighting against answering to anyone, and now I want to put his needs first. Perhaps that is the difference love creates—it makes putting someone else first easy.

Darn it. I'm going to miss dinner. Please don't be upset. I forgot to tell you I'm meeting Kat and Emma late this afternoon for a stress reduction exercise and Chinese food.

His response is delayed. Maybe I've made him mad. He can't expect me to be with him all the time. Can he? I haven't been in a relationship since our juvenile infatuation in high school. My phone beeps with an incoming message.

I'm a little disappointed, certainly not upset. I just got you back, and I'm not sure I want to share you, but enjoy your friends. Please be safe. In fact, text me when you leave and when you get to where you're going. Call me when you're ready to be picked up, and I'll come and get you. Enjoy some beef with broccoli for me. It's my favorite.

Love you,
Bobby

**PS–I'm happy to take part in stress re-
duction exercises. I have a few in mind.**

When he finds out I throw dishes to relieve
stress, he'll laugh. This exercise will help with mental
stress, but the physical type I'm happy to practice
with him.

*Thanks for being so understanding. It'll take some
time for me to get used to being us, but I like the sound
of it. Have a good day at work.*

Hugs and kisses and all the naughty stuff.

Roxy

I spend the rest of the day tidying up the messes
I've made. I want him to come home to a clean house.
My temporary presence shouldn't have to be a total
disruption to his lifestyle.

In the closet, my clothes hang on one side. He's
cleared out an entire section for me. My paltry
wardrobe takes up about ten percent of the space he
created for me.

Dressed in my new blue jeans and a black tunic,
I slip out the front door and into the elevator. My
eyes look in every direction as I leave the apartment
building. Someone *has* been following me, and it's
freaking me out. Knowing it wasn't my father's initia-
tive has caused me to feel more anxious than angry—
a feeling I don't want to entertain.

I locate the bus stop a block south and wait.
Thank goodness for smartphones. Within minutes,

my route is mapped, and I'm on my way to The Smash Shack. I really will have to get a car. Not only is riding the bus dangerous, but it's also time-consuming. I can spend several hours a day on the bus, and those are hours I could spend with Bobby.

I step off the bus. *Shoot, I forgot to text Bobby.* I take my phone from my back pocket and type an apology.

Sorry, I forgot to text when I left. I'm here at The Smash Shack safe and sound. I've been doing a lot of apologizing today.

His reply is immediate.

I worried about you. Thank you for texting. I was just getting ready to ping the GPS on your phone. No need to apologize. This is a learning curve for both of us. Call me when you're finished. I'll be there to get you. The Smash Shack, huh? I thought it was a place for angry housewives and pissed-off girlfriends. Is there anything I did I should know?

Your Bobby (More subliminal messaging)

He's so funny with his subliminal messaging. Apart from my close friends at the bar, there hasn't been a lot to laugh about in the past few years. I missed his humor—his light. I don't need to be swayed to love him. He's already in like Flynn.

Nope, you're perfection on a stick. See you tonight. We can enjoy dessert together. Wink, wink. No GPS pinging. That's just creepy and wrong.

Your Roxy

The man types fast as lightning.

I have a ravenous appetite. Looking ahead to dessert.

Your creepy Fletch

"Hey, put your phone away. It's time to break shit," Emma calls to me from down the block. She looks beautiful with her long red hair floating around her shoulders and her green eyes dancing with happiness. Right behind Emma is Kat, who also looks radiant. Both girls recently found the man of their dreams. Can the right man make you glow?

We greet each other and share hugs. Emma marches us into The Smash Shack and slaps her credit card on the counter. "We'll need a lot of dishes," she tells the girl behind the counter.

"No way. I invited you girls. I'm paying." I don't care if it takes the last dime in my account. I'm throwing shit until my mind is clear and my body aches.

"Bullshit. I'm testing out my new credit cards—my Emma Haywood cards. Anthony told me to go wild. I wouldn't want to disappoint my man." She winks at the girl behind the counter.

Geared up with gloves and goggles, we're led to a private room. The table in the back is loaded with plates, glasses, bowls, and platters. The far wall is decorated with targets. Murals of men, women, animals, and houses fill the space. Words like "hate," "love," "cheater," and "whore" are painted randomly.

The attendant goes over the safety rules and leaves us to wreak havoc.

Emma steps to the table first. She grabs a black marker and a platter and writes "COWARD" across the surface. She walks to the yellow line on the floor and lobs her plate toward the wall. It hits the man in the center of his face. Emma jumps up and down, squealing with joy.

Kat pipes in with a question. "Are you sure it's a man?"

Emma rolls her eyes. "No woman would ever cut a dress like the blue one into one-inch strips. Steal it, maybe; destroy it, never."

We consider her statement and nod.

Kat walks to the table and picks up a wineglass. In tiny letters, she writes, "Best friends should not elope." She walks to the line and tosses the glass in the air. It lands on the floor near the wall and breaks into pieces.

"I'm sorry, guys." Emma's words fade. My downcast eyes scan the floor. "Anthony didn't give me much choice. Once we were in the car, I got caught up in the moment." She looks up to find Kat laughing. "Why are you laughing?"

"I packed your bag. I knew you were getting married. I had nothing negative to write on the glass. My biggest complaint right now is Damon nagging at me to do the same. He wants his name following mine. He wants his baby in my belly."

"Oh, my God, Chris is betting Emma is already pregnant. Imagine if you both were. Talk about best friends and the stuff we do together." I glance at both of their stomachs and shake my head.

Kat walks back to the table and picks up a plate. In bold letters across the center, she writes "ANNOYING BROTHER." She takes the plate and wings it with incredible precision at the man on the wall. We join in the laughter.

I pick up a platter and scrawl "Pistachio Eating Stalker" across the front. I stand at the line and lob it at the man.

From that point on, we take turns.

"Dress Hater."

"Hangnails."

"Father."

"Couch Slasher."

"Split Ends."

"Fake Families."

We chuck dish after dish at its target. Stress recedes with every toss. When we resort to scribbling the words "body odor," "pimples," and "menstrual cramps" on the plates, it's time to go.

Laughing, we walk out together and into Lily Pond. Not too long ago, we sat in the same booth and talked about men and their madness.

CHAPTER NINETEEN

Cashew chicken, kung pao beef, and orange chicken are ordered, along with hot tea, white rice, and egg drop soup. With the necessities out of the way, let the games begin.

"First things first," Emma starts. "The insurance adjuster was out to the house today. Pretty much everything needs to be repaired or replaced. It's a large project and is going to take some time to complete. Anthony wants me to sell the house, but I won't do that until your lease runs out. I won't make you homeless." She looks at me with sad eyes.

"I appreciate that. Right now, I'm staying with Bobby, and I don't want to impose on him for too long. The faster the fixes, the better. I can stay in the house even if the contractors are there. Once my room is done,

I can be around to supervise the work." Both women look at me like I'm speaking a foreign language. "What?"

"We've both seen you with Bobby. There is no way you're an imposition. That boy is whipped."

"He's not whipped; he's in love." My white teeth flash into a huge grin.

"Oh, now you have to tell." Kat leans across the table toward me, and Emma grabs my hand. Both girls are captivated, and I have said little about anything.

"Things are good. He's sweet."

Emma throws her hands up in frustration. "You can get sweet from a candy bar. Tell us the dirty details. Is he a master in the sack? These are the important things. I can talk about candy with anyone."

"All right, all right. We made love for the first time yesterday."

Kat pipes in, "Yesterday? The prom do-over was six days ago. Cosmo says date three is the norm. What happened?"

"Oh, let's see. First, it was chivalry, then no condom, a break-in, and a meeting with dear old dad. It's like the universe was working against us, but somehow, we figured it out."

Emma groans. "Details. I want details."

"Shit... okay... he's amazing." I take a sip of my tea while contemplating my answer. "He's big... on charm, and long... on patience. His resolve is firm." Pleased with my response, I sit back and smile.

"You're a shit, Roxy Somerville." The arriving food stops the interrogation. All three of us dig into our dinners like ravenous animals. In between bites, we discuss Emma's elopement, Kat's engagement, and the break-in.

"I'm positive the break-in was about me. Do you remember the creepy guy we saw watching the house from across the street?" I eye Emma with a question in my eyes.

"Yes, but it was my dad."

"No, it wasn't. Your dad could have driven by; he might have even looked at the house a time or two, but this person stalked the house. The other day, someone knifed Bobby's tire. The break-in happened a few days later. Somehow, these things are con-nected. The bastard eats pistachios and leaves the damn shells everywhere, I'm fairly certain your fa-ther isn't such a pig. Besides, there was one in the house the night of the break-in."

The girls' mouths drop open at my statement. It's not every day someone tells you a crazy person is stalking them.

Kat speaks first. "Shit, I... Have you contacted the police?"

"Bobby knows what happened. I suppose I

should file a report, but I don't have any proof. It's a gut feeling."

Emma swallows the last of her Kung Pao chicken and exclaims, "I always go with my gut."

Kat spits out her cashew chicken. "You are so full of shit. If you trusted your gut, the fiasco with Anthony would've never happened. You knew he wasn't a cheater, and yet you tortured him and yourself."

"Yeah, but now I know he's willing to go to the ends of the earth for me. I would do the same for him. I got married in Vegas by Elvis Presley, for goodness' sake. If that doesn't shout love, then I don't know what does."

"I would've loved to be a fly on the wall." I push my dish to the side of the table and signal for the server to order beef with broccoli to go. Several minutes later, he drops off the order along with the bill and three fortune cookies. I lunge for the check and take all three fortune cookies. "You know the drill, girls. You answer a question, and you get your cookie. Eat the whole cookie before you read your fortune, or else it won't come true."

"All right, we did this last time. I'll answer first." Kat volunteers to be the first victim.

I ponder the questions bouncing in my brain. Last time, Emma asked her when the wedding would be.

"Are you considering eloping with Damon?" It's

a valid question. Often, once one friend gets married, the rest run to the altar.

Kat sits back in silence. She crosses her arms in front of her chest and blows air noisily through her mouth. "Yes, I would consider eloping. I think Emma was smart. Weddings are stressful and expensive. The only people who get to enjoy them are the guests. The couple is usually too exhausted by that point."

Kat has a point. As an event planner, she's probably seen it all.

"Oh, my gosh, I totally want to pack your bag." Emma is bubbling with joy.

"Don't pack yet and say nothing to Damon. He'll have me on the next plane to Vegas. I want to pretend at least I have a say in my wedding plans." Kat rolls her eyes before I laugh. "Give me my cookie, brat. Your turn, Em, but don't go easy on her, Roxy."

"Emma, your question is two parts. Are you trying to get pregnant, and if so, how many children do you want to have?" A devious grin breaks over her face. Emma could already be knocked up.

"That's easy to answer. I can't get pregnant because I took that damn birth control shot. So, for now, we're practicing. I don't plan to get it again. We want a family and now is as good a time as any. Besides, practicing is fun. As for how many, Anthony would probably have them until my uterus dropped out, but

I want two. One for each hand." She reaches over and grabs both cookies from me.

"Your turn." Kat and Emma whisper back and forth. Their eyes get big.

"Roxy, your question is simple. Do you love Bobby Anderson?"

"Unequivocally. It scares the crap out of me. I feel like I've known him all my life, and yet he's only been back in it less than a week. How is that possible?"

"It works that way sometimes. I heard Anthony's voice and knew. It took longer for Kat, but we're talking about Damon."

"Hey, Damon is perfect now that I have him trained. Training takes time." We all laugh.

I break and eat my cookie and wait for the others to catch up. When the cookies have been consumed, we read our fortunes and share.

I can't stop the laughter. "Mine says, 'A new pair of shoes will do you a world of good.' I own two pairs of shoes at this point in my life. A pair of blue espadrilles and a pair of silver sandals."

"Ah, Roxy, that's just temporary. I brought you a check to replace your clothes. The insurance company wants an itemized list of what was lost or destroyed, but they wrote me a check for six thousand dollars to tide us over." She reaches into her purse and pulls out a check for the entire amount made out to Roxy Somerville.

"I'm not taking the check." I push the proffered check back toward Emma. "You had more there than I did, and I didn't pay for the insurance."

"Roxanne Somerville." Emma's voice raises an octave. "I just married a billionaire. Enough said."

"Take the check, Roxy. I can vouch for Emma's financial state, and she'll be all right." Kat pulls the check from Emma's hand and shoves it across the table.

I pound my head lightly against the table. There's no use fighting these girls. Neither of them will take no for an answer. I decide to bank the money and use it to replace my bedroom furniture. Maybe I'll buy a pair of work shoes, and some more jeans and T-shirts.

"Thanks, girls. Your turn, Kat. What's your fortune say?"

Kat opens her cookie, and her mouth opens wide. "No freaking way... mine says, 'Marriage lets you annoy one special person for the rest of your life.'"

"It'll come true because you ate your cookie before you read your fortune. It's a guarantee now." Emma unfolds her fortune and howls with laughter. With a tear in her eye, she reads it. "'Life is like a bath, it's nice at first, but then you get wrinkles.' I better not get any wrinkles. I'm twenty-four years old. I've got plenty of time for wrinkles later."

I insist on paying the bill. I have a check for six thousand dollars in my purse, so I can afford dinner. Then I pull out my phone and text Bobby.

Hey Fletch,

I'm ready to come home.

Almost instantaneously, his reply arrives.

I'm ready to have you home. I'm actually parked across the street. I'll be right there.

Is he parked across the street? I told him I was going to The Smash Shack. Since the Lily Pond is almost next door, it would be a good guess.

The girls file out of the restaurant together. Bobby is waiting with a smile and a fresh bunch of daisies. I slide next to him and rise to kiss his cheek.

"Ladies. Did you have a nice dinner?" he asks, still smiling.

"Hey, Bobby." Kat smiles back at him. She looks at me and mouths the word "Whipped."

Emma moves in to hug me. She whispers in my ear, "Oh, he's got it bad for you."

With a flick of my wrist, I wave them off. They leave whispering and giggling like high school girls.

I hold up the bag for Bobby. "I brought you dinner. Isn't beef and broccoli your favorite?"

"You're a girl after my heart." He trades me the flowers for the food.

I warm inside at his thoughtful gesture. He's trying to worm his way into my heart or my pants. I'm uncertain which is his top priority. No, that's not right at all. Bobby, a twenty-four-year-old gorgeous and virile male, waited many days and didn't take up quite a few opportunities to ravish my body. As if the light bulb turns on, I realize he is after my heart.

"I thought I already had your heart. Now all I want is your body." I grab a handful of his ass and squeeze.

"Let's go home, and you can have any part of me you want." He wraps his arm around me and guides me across the street. His car is parked directly across from the restaurant.

How convenient.

"Bobby? How did you know exactly where I was?"

He looks like a boy caught taking the last cookie from the jar. "I pinged the GPS on your phone. I will not apologize. Someone has to take your safety seriously. It took me forever to hack into your signal." He gives me a *please, let's not argue,* look and walks me to the car.

"Great, now I have two stalkers. This doesn't make me happy. It's creepy and stalker-ish."

CHAPTER TWENTY

We sit in silence while Bobby starts the car and heads home. The word "stalker" sits between us. I turn to the side just in time to watch his face twitch.

"I'm not a stalker. I'm a concerned boyfriend, and someone threatened you." He releases the steering wheel and flexes his fingers. His knuckles turn from white to pink. "I want to know where you are all the time, so I know you're safe."

"No one threatened me. Someone vandalized the house. I understand the need to keep me safe. I'm concerned, too. I mean, someone has been following me, and I haven't got the foggiest idea why." My fingers brush across the soft velvet petals of the flowers in my hand.

"I'm concerned, and nothing seems to make

sense. Your dad appeared truthful, even though I believe he's a real douchebag."

"Why do you think he's truthful?" I've never known my father to lie. His honesty has been a painful part of my existence, but I haven't seen him in years, and people change.

"His secretary called with the information I requested. Your father used Eagle Investigations, and I called them today. After a considerable amount of persuasion and possibly coercion, they said the man assigned to your case was a guy named Jason." He takes a peek in my direction. "Do you know anyone named Jason Mack?"

I rack my brain for recognition. "No. The name doesn't ring a bell. In fact, I haven't met a Jason since high school."

My fingers trace the thick stems of the happy flowers. They gain their strength from their solid foundation, the same way a child thrives from growing up in a stable home. My father may have been honest, but he's never been a solid citizen or a solid family man. Who hires a private investigator to follow their daughter? Trenton Somerville, that's who.

"I tried to contact this Jason Mack. I thought he might have noticed something when he was following you. Unfortunately, he left the agency two years ago. He didn't leave a forwarding address, but

I'm trying to track him down. I'm not sure what I hope to find, but it's someplace to start."

We pull into the garage of his building and make our way upstairs. With his beef and broccoli in his hands, he heads straight for the kitchen. I follow on his heels.

"You could've joined us for dinner." I take a plate from the cupboard and set it on the counter.

He opens one container and scoops out a portion of white rice. He opens the next container and spoons the beef mixture over the rice, then closes up the boxes. "It was a girl's night out—a sacred institution."

He gets brownie points for understanding the importance of girl time. "Come here, you big hunk of burning love. How did I get so lucky to have a second chance with you?" My hands wrap around his neck, bringing his face to mine.

"You have an angel of a friend named Emma." He presses his lips to mine and retreats. With his loaded plate in his hands, he walks to the living room and settles on the couch.

"That angel told me Anthony wants her to sell the house." I plop on the couch next to him with a pout on my face.

"Really?" He pops a forkful of food in his mouth.

"She said she wouldn't consider it until my lease expired. I hate to force her to keep the house. I can find a new place to live." With my feet on the coffee table, I make myself comfortable. "It's a shame because I love that house. I could live there for years."

Bobby swallows his food. "What makes the house so special?"

I rock my head side to side, trying to come up with the right words. "It feels like home. Don't get me wrong, I appreciate you opening your home to me, but this is your home. It's not mine." Everything about Emma's house is perfect. It's the house I was living in when Bobby came back into my life.

His face falls, and my heart sinks. I've hurt his feelings.

"This is temporary." He sweeps his fork-filled hand around the room. "We can get a place of our own."

He's ready to dive into the deep end. It's easy to love a man who's willing to do whatever it takes to make me happy. It's easy to love him. That thought gives me a change of heart. Don't they say home is where the heart is? My heart is happily mingling with Bobby's right here in his little one-bedroom apartment. "You know what? I'm happy here. I'll be happy wherever you are." That's actually the truth, too.

"You've had to settle for several years because one man disappointed you. I won't be the second.

We'll find a place that's perfect for us." He kicks off his shoes and slides his feet next to mine on the table.

"Just love me for me. It's all I've ever needed. It's all I want." I snuggle into his side, pick a piece of broccoli from his plate, and pop it into my mouth.

"Despite your thievery," he pulls his plate from my reach, "I do love you. I love everything you bring to my life, and wherever you are is where I want to be."

"You're too easy, mister. You need to learn to make me work for it."

"Haven't you been working hard enough? Love should be easy, Roxy. Loving you is easy." He sets his plate on the table and wraps me in his arms.

Is it supposed to be this easy?

I WAKE UP EARLY, my body naked and warm next to his. This is what home feels like. Falling asleep in his arms is perfect, but waking next to him is better. I slip from the room. No clothes are in sight. I don't want to wake him, so I head to the kitchen naked as the day I was born.

There, I rinse my mouth in the sink. I pull out the checkered apron from the drawer, slide the strap over my head, and wrap the skirt around my center. The cloth covers almost everything. My breasts spill out the sides, and my bottom catches a breeze when I move too quickly.

I whip up a frittata and brew a pot of coffee. Breakfast cools on the stovetop while I wash the dishes.

A whistle sounds behind me.

"It doesn't get any better than this. I've read about women naked in the kitchen, but I never imagined it to be so—"

"Stop. I'm not naked." I pull at the bib of the apron. It's no use; there isn't enough material to cover my chest. "I wanted to surprise you with breakfast."

"It's definitely a surprise." His eyes skate over my body.

I turn away so he can't ogle my boobs.

"That's a good view, too."

My hands snap to my behind to make sure the fabric is closed. His laughter reverberates around the room.

"Stop teasing me." My voice booms. I try to sound angry, but the whole situation lends itself to humor, and I give up and laugh.

He closes his mouth, but the laughter is in his eyes. "I'm not teasing you. I love this." Dressed in sweatpants and a T-shirt, he closes in on me. Pinned against the counter, he nuzzles my neck. "Thanks for breakfast. Today will go down as one of the best mornings of my life."

My hands run up his chest. "What was the absolute best morning?"

"That's easy. It was the first morning you woke up in my arms."

He knows exactly how to melt a girl's heart. I press my body into him, and all thoughts of breakfast are gone. Morning sex is a perfect way to start the day.

DRESSED in Bobby's sweatpants and T-shirt, I heat his breakfast while he finishes his shower. He'll be late for work if he doesn't hurry. We're going to have to fine-tune our schedules if we plan to insert extracurricular activities into our daily lives. Sex done right shouldn't be rushed.

He zips out of the bedroom, dressed and ready to go. It's a scene right out of a movie. I hand him his keys, a paper plate with a wedge of frittata, and a mug of coffee. He leans over to kiss me.

"Bye, dear." I bat my eyelashes at him and smile.

He stops a few steps from the door, bends over, and places the paper plate and the mug on the floor. He shoves the keys into his pocket and approaches me. "I love you. Be safe today. I'll pick you up at work tonight." His lips press against mine. We get lost in the kiss.

I pull away. "Go. I don't want you to get in trouble." I pick up his breakfast and put it in his hands. Turning him toward the hallway, I swat his firm ass as he walks away.

Back in the apartment, I look around for things to do. Bobby is a very tidy man and keeps his home spotless. In the bedroom, I pull at my side of the covers. We destroyed this bed last night and this morning, and I smile at the memory of his body covering mine. We aren't getting a lot of rest these days. I have the time to sleep another couple of hours, so I take my phone from the nightstand and send Bobby a message.

You wore me out. I'm going back to sleep for a few hours.

Your Firefly

I wore you out? My ass is dragging, but it was worth every lost minute of sleep. Sweet dreams. Be safe.

Your one true love, Fletch (subliminal messaging :-))

I smile at his message and realize loving him is the right thing for me. I nod off with thoughts of Bobby floating through my head. Never have I felt so safe or loved in my life.

Three hours later, I pop awake—my body covered in sweat and my heart beating through my chest. The dream was terrifying. The hoodie-wearing, pistachio-eating man took me. I couldn't see his face, but he was familiar. Though I tried to escape, I wasn't strong enough. He held me from behind. I panicked in my dream because I was unprepared—unprotected.

To warm my chilled body, I climb into a hot shower. Still fresh in my mind, the dream has me contemplating ways I could've protected myself. I could've used the skills Bobby taught me the other day, but fear paralyzed me. Fear made it impossible for me to think clearly. I scold myself for taking the dream too seriously.

It was a dream, for God's sake.

Still, it was so real.

Dressed in black jeans, a new pair of boots, and a button-down cotton shirt, I walk out the door and head to work. Tonight should fly by—it's Friday, and all the partiers will come out to play. Once I finish my shift, I'll be back in Bobby's arms.

The front of the bus seems safer, so I tuck myself in the seat behind the driver. Bobby asked me to take a cab, but I couldn't justify the cost. Years ago, I wouldn't have blinked at tossing down hundreds of dollars for a driver. Now, thirty dollars for a cab gives me heart palpitations.

The night gets off to a busy start. There's a pre-wedding party. When two men get married, do they have a bachelor party or a bachelorette party? Either way, the group is having a blast. Round after round of Dew Mes are ordered. It's a tasty mix of Midori liqueur, Triple sec, pineapple juice, and a splash of Mountain Dew.

With two bartenders on duty, everything is going smoothly. The raucous laughter of the wedding group draws my attention to their corner. One man has a top hat, the other a veil, and they are too damn funny.

My thoughts drift to Chris and Trevor. Will they tie the knot? If so, Chris will wear the satin, and Trevor will select everything because he has better taste by far. While I envision my friends' nuptials, the empty bar seats have filled in with a few regulars.

"Hey, Tommy, draft or bottle tonight?" Tommy is an older man. One would never think of him as gay, but I've seen him hook up a time or two. He works in the financial district as some kind of planner. He's always asking me to let him look at my portfolio, but I don't have money to invest.

"Draft tonight. How are things with you, Roxy?"

"It's been a busy week." I recite the new and noteworthy events in my life. "I have a fabulous new boyfriend. Someone vandalized my house, so I'm now staying with said boyfriend. I met with my dad for the first time in four years. So, yeah, I'd say it's been a full week." I draw the beer and set it in front of him. "What about you?"

"I was out of town for a few days. My niece had a child—a boy. They named him Emory. What do you think of that name?" He takes a drink of his beer. His tongue slides out to lick the foam from his lips. "All I can say is, the kid better learn to fight at an early age."

Why do parents saddle their kids with crazy names? Roxanne was bad enough after the Eddie Murphy movie showed him singing "Roxanne" in prison. Ever since then, Roxanne has been synonymous with a girl with loose morals.

"I don't know, Tommy. Parents do silly shit with names. There's nothing wrong with a common name."

"What would you name your child?"

That's an interesting question. I never thought I would have children. The thought of being a parent frightens the hell out of me. Would I be like my parents? However, now that Bobby is in my life, I can see the possibilities. A little boy with green eyes is a beautiful thought.

"I would go with something traditional, like Robert, or Mark, or maybe even Thomas. Those are strong names nobody will mess with." There is a movement to my left. Mason has arrived and sits in my section of the bar. "I've got to run, Tommy. Let me know when you need a refill."

I hurry to the center of the bar and smile. Mason looks messy. His whiskers have filled in since the last time I saw him. It's only been a few days, but it seems like weeks.

"Hey, Roxa—Roxy."

I smile at his effort.

"Scotch on the rocks?"

I pull the tumbler from the shelf. When he nods, I scoop in a few cubes and pour three fingers of the caramel-colored liquor into the glass.

"How are things?" His tone carries a hint of curiosity.

"I can't complain. Well, I could, but it doesn't do me any good. So, I'll just go with the flow."

"What happened that you could complain about?" He sips his drink and looks at me over the edge of his glass.

"Not much. My house was broken into the other day. The damage was so severe that I had to move out temporarily. It appears I have a stalker. One who likes pistachio nuts."

His eyes grow large. "You're kidding me? That's awful. What's wrong with people these days?" He sets his glass down and picks up the paper napkin.

Wondering if he might fold me another flower, my eyes never leave the paper in his hand. He surprises me by shredding it into strips, then slicing each strip into confetti-like squares.

"Are you feeling a little stressed yourself?" I look at the pile of pink in front of him.

"Yes, I am. The church can't loan me the room for self-defense classes any longer. I have to find a new place to work."

"That's not your only source of income, is it?" I know what it feels like to be displaced. Without Bobby, I would be in a world of hurt.

"No, I'm a private investigator. I work as an independent contractor."

"It's a small world. My boyfriend is a detective, but he got his start working for a private detective agency." My pride must show in my smile because Mason smiles back at me.

"Is that right?"

"Yes, so... what kind of cases do you work on?" I lean against the bar. With a glance, I make sure everyone is taken care of in my section.

"Mostly divorce, cheating spouses, that sort of thing. I've done a missing person or two. I also get a lot of insurance fraud cases. I lurk in corners and take pictures of injured people doing activities they shouldn't."

The word "lurk" sends a chill up my spine. It's crazy that people hire others to stalk someone. "Doesn't it feel creepy to shadow someone?"

"It pays the bills." He shrugs and goes back to sipping his drink.

I walk away, shaking my head. Sometimes, a line has to be drawn between right and wrong.

Hiding in corners and secretly following people is wrong.

Tommy raises his glass, showing he's ready for a refill.

"Who's the guy you were talking with? I like them rough and grizzly looking. Care to introduce me?" I place his beer in front of him and tell him to follow me down the bar.

Once I arrive in front of Mason, I begin the introductions.

"Mason, this is my friend, Tommy. He asked me to introduce you to him." Mason's head snaps back as if I'd slapped him. *What an odd reaction.* He looks toward Tommy, and a smile spreads across both men's faces. Mason offers his weathered hand to shake.

I leave the two men to get acquainted with one another. I wouldn't have picked them to pair up, but stranger couplings have occurred. I make the rounds and find Chris and Trevor hanging out with the drunk wedding party.

"Hey, boys."

Chris looks at me but ignores my greeting. He turns to Trevor and talks loudly enough for me to hear. "I'm not sure we should talk to her anymore. She had a girl's night out and didn't invite us." Chris harrumphs and turns his head away from me.

"Oh, puhlease, it was a no-boyfriends night. Considering neither of you has a vagina who was I to invite, and who would I leave out? Next time you can both come, but prepare to giggle and gossip."

Trevor reaches over and pinches my cheek. "You are so cute when you're irritated. As far as giggles, that would be Chris's department." He lovingly tweaks Chris's nose. "Did you have a good time? I love the Lily Pond. They have the best moo goo gai pan in town."

"Yes, we had a great time, but I'm more of an orange chicken girl myself." We chat for a few more minutes before I run off to check on the bar. I glance over at Mason and Tommy, and they are deep in conversation. It's nice to see Mason interacting with someone since he's usually alone.

The other bartender shouts, "Last call." I look at the clock above the bar. The night has flown by like I'd thought it would. I set off to fill my last orders and stock the bar so I can be out of here as soon as the bar closes.

The last patron stumbles from the building, his sober friend guiding him through the door. I race around, wiping off tables and sweeping the floor. Several minutes later, I shout goodbye to my coworker and race to Bobby.

CHAPTER TWENTY-ONE

Over the next few weeks, we settle into a routine, early morning wake-up for Bobby and late-night pickups for me. We spend our nights making love and our days making plans. But I can tell Bobby is up to something because he has a devious smile on his face most days.

"Hey, it's been really quiet. Maybe my dad lied about having me followed. Doesn't it seem odd as soon as we talked to him, everything stopped?" I drag the hairbrush through my tangled mass of hair.

"It's a strange coincidence for sure. I still want you to remain alert to your surroundings." He stands behind me and combs his hair. We have mastered the dance of being in the bathroom at the same time. His height gives him an edge.

I pull my hair into a ponytail and pinch my cheeks for color. I'm as ready as I'll ever be to meet his mom.

"Don't be nervous. My mom will love you." He turns me around to face him. "It's just lunch."

When he talked about me meeting his mother, I assumed he meant in the distant future. As soon as I said I'd love to meet her—a figure of speech, by the way—He scheduled the date for our first available Saturday—today.

I really want to meet his mom. However, I'm a bit gun shy with parents. Mine wouldn't get the parent of the year award, and I had little exposure to other parents. I prefer to tell people wolves raised me. It's closer to the truth.

"I'm not nervous. I'm petrified. I don't do parents."

His eyes are full of compassion as he genuinely understands my fear. "You'll love my mom. She insisted on cooking, and she even asked what you like to eat. I told her penis." He stares at me, trying not to laugh.

My mouth drops open. "You're impossible." I slug him lightly in the chest.

"I told her you love anything that will grease your arteries or rot your teeth." He pivots and walks out of the bathroom, laughing as he goes. I follow.

Both answers are honest. Only one is acceptable.

I may love to eat his penis, but he better never tell his mother. One whisper in that direction and I'll bite it off the next time I'm down there.

"You make it sound like I dip tortillas in lard for breakfast, lunch, and dinner. I eat vegetables. I ate your fabulous egg white omelets, and I even tried quinoa. I'm not a fan, but I gave it a solid effort." I've been trying to cook healthier for his benefit.

"Tortillas are lard mixed with a sprinkling of flour." He holds my hand as we walk out the door together.

I insist on stopping by the florist. One of the few words of worthy wisdom my mother taught me was to never go to someone's house empty-handed. I can't decide on the type of flower, so I buy a large mixed arrangement.

His mother lives a few miles away. My parents would've said it's the other side of the tracks, but having lived in West Hollywood for several months, it's a great place to be. Bobby's childhood home sits on a tree-lined street just blocks from Beverly Hills. It's how we met. He may have lived in West Hollywood, but he went to Beverly Hills High School.

We pull in front of the yellow house, and I take a big breath and straighten my skirt as I exit the car. I have the fight-or-flight instinct beating heavily in my head. Bobby recognizes the fear on my face, and he cups my cheek with his palm and lightly kisses my lips.

"I love you, Roxanne Somerville, and my mother will, too."

Feeding off his confidence, I stand tall and make my way to the door. We barely reach it before it flies open, and Bobby's mom reaches out to hug me.

"Come in... come in... I've been waiting for you two to show up."

"Mom, we're early. You said noon; it's fifteen minutes before our scheduled arrival time."

"Oh, shush, I'm excited to have you two over for lunch. It's not every day my son calls and tells me he's in love."

My face flies up to look at Bobby. He winks at me and blows me a kiss. *Oh, I might have to kill him later.* All of those self-defense lessons he's been giving me might come in handy when I need to kick his ass tonight.

"Roxy, this is my mom, Theresa. Mom, this is Roxy." A modern-day June Cleaver stands before me. Happiness bubbles from her every pore. She's exuberant and looks at her son with love and pride. Lovely green eyes smile with warmth, the same eyes as Bobby. It's not there the resemblance ends; he's blessed with her generosity of spirit as well.

With the formal introductions made, Theresa guides us into the kitchen. I hand her the bouquet,

and she gushes over the flowers. Maybe this afternoon won't be so painful. I expected to feel awkward.
Instead, I feel at ease—another place where the
thought of home seems comforting.

Bobby pulls out a chair next to the whitewashed
table, and the initials of several people are carved into
the top: BA, TA, DA, and MA mar the finish. In the
center is a heart with the initials KA. I look up at
Bobby with a question in my eyes.

"Kevin Anderson is my dad. I haven't said much
about him because I never got to know him. My mom
has tried to keep him alive by telling us stories. I was
two when he passed away. The twins were one." The
information is factual, not emotional.

"How did you raise three boys by yourself?" My
mother had a staff to raise her three kids. Theresa did
it all on her own.

"I did what I had to do. I didn't have a choice,"
she said.

"It's been so long. Why haven't you remarried?"

"Kevin was my one true love. We met in high
school. I married him the day I turned eighteen. We
waited a few years to have children. I was twenty-two
when I had Bobby and twenty-three when I gave
birth to the twins, Douglas and Michael. My husband died in a car accident on the 405. I hate that
damned freeway."

I trace over the letters carved with love. They no

longer appear to mar the surface but decorate it with the force of binding love.

"See, love at first sight. It's a real thing, Roxy." He places his hand over mine as I trace his initials.

"The love bug has bitten my boy. What about you? Do you love my boy?" Theresa opens the oven and pulls out a delicious-looking roast. Sprinkled around the edge of the pan are carrots, potatoes, and onions. Scented steam rises from the pan, tickling my nose.

"Mom, Roxy comes from a family who doesn't show affection the same way we do. She's more re-served than we are." He squeezes my hand.

"She'll get used to us. We'll have her spouting sonnets in no time. One thing is for certain, Roxy, the Anderson men are persistent. When they decide you're it, there's no changing their minds. Weren't you two an item in high school? If I remember cor-rectly, my son swooned the day he met you."

"I didn't swoon. I don't swoon, Mother. May I help you set the table?"

Bobby's retort makes me giggle. Grateful for the distraction, I offer to help. His mother catches my at-tention and mouths the word "Swoon" behind his back. We continue to laugh and set the small table for three, then sit down for lunch.

Conversation during lunch goes back and forth between funny stories of Bobby growing up and

Theresa's memories of her husband, Kevin. Bobby has a lot in common with his long-deceased father. He's passionate, generous, and committed. After we clean the kitchen from lunch, Theresa sends Bobby to her room to get a picture of his father. While he's gone, she looks at me and says, "You love my son. It's in your eyes. Make sure you tell him. He needs to hear it from you." She pauses briefly. "I miss those three words. I wish I could've heard them once more."

I reach across the table and set my hand over Theresa's. It's my silent way of telling her I understand.

My love for Bobby must be written all over my face if his mother sees it. My heart knows it, but my mouth won't say it. Once it's out, I can't take it back. *What are you afraid of?* Tonight, while we make love, I'll tell him. He deserves to hear the words my heart screams.

Bobby returns with the picture of his dad. They could be twins. His dad died at twenty-five, which is almost the same age as Bobby now. The thought of losing him makes me feel nauseous. To lose your love at such a young age would be awful. How does a young wife recover?

"How did you survive? I can't imagine going forward after what you lost."

Could I go on, or would I shrivel up and die? My

resolve is firm. I lost my entire family and survived, but losing Bobby would be worse. The thought hollows me out.

"I had to go on. My boys were counting on me. Kevlar would have been disappointed in me if I gave up. That's how he got his nickname. He always seemed bulletproof. His friends called him Kevlar once he fell from the second-story window after a drinking binge in high school." Her eyes light at the memory. "That boy bounced up and walked back inside to down a few more beers."

"What did Mr. Anderson call you?" I figure Theresa had to have had a nickname. "Bobby calls me Firefly. Are nicknames a family tradition?"

"Nicknames are a sign of affection. Kev called me Peaches. I'm not telling you why. We'll leave it at that. Breast cancer picked my fruit too early." She winks at me while Bobby groans.

"Mom, I so didn't need to hear that."

"You're a grown man, Bobby, and I'm sure you've had your share of perfectly ripe peaches." His mother lets out a laugh that comes from her gut. It's full and rich and makes me smile.

"I have a customer at work who tells me I'm a lotus flower. I hope it's not a sign of affection. I thought it was weird because he said something about rising from the darkness or the mud or something similar. When he explained I was finding myself in the world, it made more sense. Telling someone we rise from the murky waters to become new again didn't sound flattering at first."

"Who called you a lotus flower?" Bobby doesn't look happy.

"Just this guy who comes into the bar. His name is Mason. He's the guy I told you about who teaches self-defense. He used to hold classes at the church, but he got booted for some reason. His actual job is a private investigator, or so he says." Bobby looks to be logging all of this information away. Is he jealous because someone else gave me a nickname? Men are so funny. "You have nothing to worry about. He's gay. I introduced him to a man a couple of weeks ago, and he hasn't been in since. Maybe they ran off into the sunset together."

His mother breaks into the conversation with, "I love nicknames. Do you have one for Bobby?" His mom tilts her head to the side and waits for a response.

"I call him Fletch after his love of all things Jessica Fletcher. It's a good thing he wasn't a fan of Magnum P.I.; people would assume he was named after a condom." The words slide out of my mouth before I can take them back. Did I just use the word "condom" in front of his mother?

Lord, I need to get a filter.

"Magnum is about right." Bobby smiles.

His mother slaps him on the side of the head. We all break into laughter. What started out as a day destined to be stressful turned into one of the highlights of my adult life. Who knew parents could be so much fun? His mom was warm and welcoming and open and honest. For the second time today, I wanted to tell someone else I love you. What's not to love about Theresa Anderson? She brought Bobby into this world.

We hug and kiss at the door. Theresa makes us promise to visit again soon. The look in her eyes says she's going into the house to name her grandchildren.

Bobby walks me to my side of the car. "My mom loves you. I knew she would."

He rubs his hands down my sides. The soft strokes of his fingers vibrate across my skin. The pressure of his fingertips wakes up my sensitive parts. I wish we had time for a quick roll in the sheets, but sadly we stayed at his mom's house longer than planned, and now there was just enough time to change into jeans and go straight to work.

"I love your mom. When you talked about being in love, I wanted to throttle you. Most moms don't like their son's choices in women. Your mom is amazing. She made me feel like part of the family."

"You are part of the family. We just haven't ironed out the details yet." He takes advantage of my open mouth and slides his tongue between my lips.

The kiss is so full of passion, it nearly buckles my knees. "Let's get you home and changed. I don't want to make you late for work. I mean, I do want to make you late for work, but I won't." He opens the door and helps me into the car. Glancing back at his mom's house, I see Theresa smile and wave from the window.

We make it home and back to the car in record time. It's a good thing Bobby stayed in the kitchen while I changed. We might not have made it out of the bedroom if he didn't. Once we made love, it was as if neither one could get enough of the other.

"I'm heading out tonight with some guys from the precinct. We're playing pool and having a few beers. I'll be there waiting for you when you get off." He walks me to the bar entrance and kisses me goodbye.

"Have fun. If you drink too much, take a cab home. I can get home on my own."

I turn to look at him. His eyes twinkle when he looks at me. I've never felt so loved in my life. I blow him a kiss just before the door closes.

CHAPTER TWENTY-TWO

Saturday nights at Trax are never dull. Tonight is drag night, and I've never seen so many beautiful men dressed as women. Hell, the men make better-looking women than some women do. How do they get such a close shave on their faces? A lovely brunette grabs my attention. Fire Down Under is painted perfectly across his plump lips. The color brings back memories.

It's the same color I bought the day we went lingerie shopping. The sexy demi-cup bra, garters, and hose still sit unused in my drawer. They haven't made their debut since naked is our dress code. Clothes fall off the minute the door shuts.

I used red lipstick once. I slicked it on, intending to leave a ring around him. I gave him a blowjob the last time he went out with the boys. If he considered cheating on me, which I'm sure he wouldn't, I wanted to make sure I put a ring on him. One on his finger would be great, but the one I left wouldn't be easy to take off. The red pigment can last for days. It was essential to mark my territory.

Perhaps it was time to bring out the sexy lingerie. Painting my lips fiery red, I'll make it a night he'll remember for years to come. He won't doubt my love. It's all about him for me now.

Preoccupied with thoughts of the night to come, I work on autopilot. I look up and see Tommy sitting at the bar. I pour him a draft beer and sidle up to the bar to chat.

"How are you, Tommy? You haven't been around in a while."

"I was staying away." His eyes look around the room. "I thought Mason and I had hit it off a few weeks ago. We left together. I moved in for a kiss, and he punched me." He winces as his hand slides over his left eye. There is a trace of a yellow-green shadow above his cheekbone. "I was sporting a shiner the size of Maine for nearly two weeks. I finally came out of hiding. Thank goodness I can work from home. I didn't want to answer a bunch of questions." He lowers his head and looks into his beer.

"Oh, my goodness. He hit you? I can't believe it.

I'm so sorry I introduced the two of you." I'm morti-
fied that I started this whole mess.

"I asked you to introduce us. This isn't your fault.
Maybe I moved too quickly for him." He shrugs and
takes a sip of his beer.

"That was wrong. When you leave a bar with
someone, there's sort of an expectation. He should
have known you were interested in him. It would've
been obvious what you were interested in."

Tommy waves my comment off. He tips back his
beer and downs it. I draw him another one and leave
to check on the other patrons. My foot catches on
something and slides across the floor, and I nearly
landed on my butt. Whatever I stepped on felt like a
marble. Afraid someone might slip and hurt themselves, I go in search of the nefarious object.

Light gleams on a white object on the floor. *Is it a
button?* A man dancing in a red dress kicks it.
Carmen Miranda, he isn't, but he has excellent taste
in shoes. I follow the object to its stopping point in
the corner. With two fingers, I pick up what looks
like a small stone. My heart nearly stops. It's an intact
pistachio nut.

My eyes move around the room. I go from table
to table, looking for shells, hoping the one in my hand
belongs to one of the drag queens. It's hard to fear a
drag queen. As I round the room, I approach the bar.

Tommy is gone, and in his place is a handful of nuts spread across the bar where he sat.

Blood rushes to my head, drowning out the sound of the music. The *thump, thump, thump* of my heart in my ears is deafening. Could it be Tommy? Nothing would make me believe he could do any of the things that had happened to me. What would be his endgame? He's a well-off financial planner. Did I make him angry when I didn't have him supervise my portfolio? I have no money to invest. It makes little sense.

I look across the bar while my coworker flags me down. I walk to him in a daze. "Where did Tommy go?" My voice rises with panic. "Is he still here?"

"No, he tossed a ten on the counter and left abruptly. He was acting weird, like he was hiding something. I've never seen him like that. It's totally out of character." He reaches under the counter and takes out a wrapped package. "Some guy dropped this off and said he'd see you soon." He pushes the package toward me and walks away.

The only man I'm seeing soon is Bobby, so I smile at his gift. His timing is perfect. He probably ran in and then ran out as soon as he saw all the men dressed in their finest. Maybe Tommy saw him and freaked out. If he's been following me, then he would have seen Bobby and me together. Bobby's height alone is intimidating. Add his muscular build, and most men want to keep their distance.

I rip into the paper to find a box. My mouth goes dry the instant I lift the top off. Inside are his trophies. A piece of football, a scrap of a blue dress, and a bit of silicone from my vibrator. Little scraps of items stolen over time. An earring that went missing months ago sits on a bed of unshelled pistachio nuts. Letters upon letters from my mother and sisters fill the box. Feeling as if I might faint, I slide down the bar to the floor.

"Are you all right? You don't look well," my co-worker says. "Go home. I've got this. People are leaving, anyway. Only the diehards will stay until closing." He helps me from the floor and points me to the door.

My brain processes two words. Go home. Yes, that's what I'll do. I'll go home where it's safe. Where Bobby can hold me and make it all better. I pull my phone from my pocket. Trying to suppress the panic, I text him a message.

Bobby, he's been here. The pistachio man. He's been here, and I need you. Please come and get me.

His response is immediate.

Stay put. I'm on my way.

The heat from the dancing crowd makes me ill. I need air, fresh air, right now. I slam the lid on the box, tuck it under my arm, and bolt out the door. I stumble right into a concrete chest.

"Oomph," escapes my mouth, and the box falls from my hands. Pistachio nuts dance across the sidewalk. Strong hands keep me on my feet, and relief washes over me. He got here fast.

"Bobby, you came." I raise my eyes, but his pools of green don't stare down at me. Dark slate, the color of hate and anger, meets my gaze.

"Mason, what are you doing here?"

"We have unfinished business." His voice is full of malicious intent. The lump in my throat nearly chokes me. Is he the stalker? All this time and he's been right in front of me.

His grip is painful. Roughened, knobby fingers dig into my flesh. Propelled forward, he shoves me into a black Jeep, idling by the curb. A plastic tie tightens around my wrists, burrowing into my tender skin, while bile rises in my throat. I should've fought. I should've followed Bobby's safety lessons to kick, hit, or poke his eyes. Fear washes over me like a tsunami. I scream, but no one comes to help.

"Help... help me." I press my face to the window while I scream.

A woman walking down the sidewalk raises an eyebrow. Mason steps in front of the window and laughs. "My wife had a bit much tonight." He makes an *I'm crazy* motion with his finger, orbiting his ear.

The woman giggles and walks away. Surely, she must not know Trax is a gay bar. He rounds the car and opens the driver's door to climb inside.

I shift in my seat, pull up my feet, and kick. My right foot painfully hits the gearshift, my left foot connecting with his head.

"Damn it. You stupid bitch." The words spill from his mouth while he subdues me.

The tie he'd placed cuts into my ankles. He shoves me back into the seat. My head hits painfully against the glass, but it's panic that makes me dizzy.

Calm down, I tell myself. Bobby told me a calm brain is a thinking brain.

Breathe.

Bobby will come.

Think.

I shift to sit up in the seat. My restrained hands brush across my pocket. *My phone.* If I can get my phone out, I may have a chance. I wiggle the phone from my jeans as the car moves forward. Wedging it into the crease of the seat, I sit back and pray he doesn't find it. Thank goodness it's on silent. Any text or sound would've been a dead giveaway.

Maybe Mason is a crappy private investigator. If he doesn't consider my phone, I'll be lucky. Bobby will try to track it. He hasn't given up his stalker tendencies, which at this moment makes me very thankful.

"Why me? Why have you been following me for years?" I twist and turn in my seat. My side glides across the smooth door. The handles have been removed, leaving me trapped, with no way to escape.

Shit.

Shit.

Shit.

"Why not?" He shrugs his shoulders. "It started as a job. It turned into an opportunity. You're a hobby."

He picks up a nut from a cup in his console. The shell cracks between his teeth. He spits it toward my side of the floor and chews the meaty nut inside. My feet slide across the littered floor, and there must be hundreds of shells beneath me.

His matter-of-fact tone chills me—a *hobby. Am I a damn hobby?*

"I'm a job? My father hired you." It's a statement of fact. "Is he aware of what you're doing?" The pitch of my voice rises, along with my fear. "He can't be okay with you kidnapping me."

"No, your father gave up too easily. I'm in it for the long haul. Imagine what he'll give me if I can deliver him an obedient daughter?"

The information sits like lead in my belly. He thinks he can make me behave. Somehow, he thinks I have value to my father.

"He won't give you anything. He's washed his

hands of me, you idiot." His backhanded slap leaves a sting so deep, I feel it on the other side of my face. Tears spring from my eyes. I've never been hit before.

"I won't stand for your insolence. It's what started this in the first place. You have a sharp tongue and a spirited nature I intend to tame." He pulls to the side of the road and tosses my purse out the window. Reaching toward me, he pats down my pockets. "Where's your phone? It's always in your back pocket."

My mouth drops open. His intimate knowledge of me is frightening. "I dropped it with the box when you attacked me outside the bar." My voice wavers. Tears stream freely down my face. "I had it in my hand. I was calling for a ride."

A sinister smile crosses his face.

A joyous smile hides behind my look of horror. If he doesn't find my phone, I have a chance of surviving.

After a thorough pat-down, he pulls onto the highway and drives forward. "I didn't attack you; I escorted you. There's a difference. You'll know when you're being attacked." His voice holds a promise of things to come. "You could've tried to defend yourself if you'd taken my class."

"Did you really teach classes?" I have a hard time believing anything he says. "Is your name even Mason?"

"Nope, I'm Jason Mack. I just switched it around so no one could trace me. Clever, huh?" He continues to suck the salt off the pistachios. He cracks them and spits the empty shells my way.

"And the classes?"

"Yep, I taught self-defense. One girl complained I was too rough, and the church tossed me on my ass. Aren't we supposed to turn the other cheek and all that? The girl was a menace. If you want to look like a whore and dress like a whore, then you'll probably get treated like a whore."

"Why try to teach women if you don't like them?" I need the information to make good decisions. "Do you have a wife, a daughter?"

His hands tighten on the steering wheel. The glow from the streetlights shines on his white knuckles while the reflection of the dash illuminates his stony expression.

Shit, I hit a nerve.

"Not anymore." He cackles like a crazy person.

Dare I ask more? I need to know what happened to his wife.

"Are you divorced?"

"Yep, she wouldn't behave, so I had to do what was necessary. Shut up and rest. You're going to need your energy."

Not wanting to contact from the back of his hand again, I comply with his wish and close my mouth.

The mile markers float by while the city lights dim in the distance. We wind our way into the mountains. As the air chills, my hope fades. This man isn't giving up until I'm tamed or dead, and judging by how I struggled to stay composed now, I could easily succumb to fear.

Bobby told me weeks ago, the only thing I can control is the moment I'm in. I can give in to fear, or I can fight back. I've never been one to cave to pressure. I've been a fighter all my life. I've fought for control for years, so there is no way I'm relinquishing it to a crazy man. I'll play along until an opportunity presents itself.

Come on, Bobby, present yourself.

CHAPTER TWENTY-THREE

We arrive at a cabin in the woods. He pulls me from the car and leans me against the hood. I listen; the silence of the night is deafening. The hoot of an owl splinters the quiet while the wind rustles through the woods. The pitch-black of the night is dotted with streams of moonlight as it peeks through the canopy of trees. "Desolate" is the word filling my mind.

Breathe.

I inhale the fresh air, hoping a dose of courage and wisdom will enter my body with every breath.

Think.

I take in my surroundings. If I can set myself free, I can get lost in the woods. I would rather perish trying to escape than stay and die his captive.

He cuts the tie around my ankles. As soon as

they're released, I kick and scream. I connect hard with his shin. I feel no pain because adrenaline is an excellent anesthetic. My fight is in vain, though, because he grabs me when I try to run away.

His hand grips my long hair. With an aggressive tug, he drags me toward the cabin, kicking and screaming. I swear I can hear the pounding of my heart for miles.

He unlocks the door and shoves me inside. I stumble and fall. The rough wood floor rips through my jeans and into my flesh, and I cry out in pain.

So much for adrenaline.

He strikes a match and lights a lantern, and the room glows to life.

One room.

No windows.

One door.

Deadbolt.

Hope vanishes. "Bleak" is the word filling my mind now. Bobby's voice is in my head, telling me it's never over until it's over.

Breathe.

Opportunities will present themselves.

Think.

He'll slip up, and when he does, I'll be ready.

He looms over my prone body. With a pull of my shoulder, he flips me onto my back. I grimace at the pain in my hands. The weight of my body crushing them makes them throb.

"Let's get one thing clear. You're in the middle of nowhere, and we are so off the grid. Finding you will be like finding Waldo. The faster you learn to behave, the better. Your father is a stickler for perfection. I won't deliver anything but a paragon of perfect behavior."

"My father is not interested in getting me back." Maybe I can talk some sense into the man. He's not a man I can sway with emotions, but perhaps logic will work.

"Your father is used to getting what he wants. He's not a man to settle or give up."

His rough hands lift me to my feet and shove me into the rickety wooden chair sitting alone in the center of the room. I look down at my knee, and blood is oozing from the wound. Pushing the pain aside, I scan my surroundings. Off to the right is a table with a camp stove, water bottles, canned food, and an opener. A large cardboard box sits to the left. It's the size of a wardrobe and big enough for a body. My eyes grow large. Does he plan to keep me here?

He follows my eyes to the box and laughs.

"It's a toilet. It's the only privacy you'll get."

"How long do you plan to keep me?"

"As long as it takes, my lotus flower. I will pull you from the darkness. You will rise and be pure once more. I can't remove the stain of the men who have used you, but I can convince you that falling in line with your father's wishes will benefit you. Fathers always know best." He turns and walks away.

"Screw you."

I didn't mean to say the words out loud, and I regret them as soon as they slip past my lips. He swings back around, grasps a handful of hair, and yanks my head back. My vertebrae pop. He's pulled several chunks of hair free from my scalp. They float to the floor in front of me.

"There's that smart mouth of yours again. You're a Somerville, Roxanne. Act like one. If you can't remember how to behave, I'll be happy to show you."

I freeze. Roxanne. That's why he called me Roxanne. Bastard. He pushes my head forward and releases me. My scalp throbs in several places. I swear my head must be bleeding where he tore the hair from it.

Two choices, that's all I have. I can surrender and hope for the best or go with my original plan and fight to the death. I decide to behave for the time being. If I can get him to release my hands, I'll have more options.

"I'm sorry. It's just my hands hurt. The ties are cutting off my circulation. The pain is making me cranky."

I try to look contrite. Deep inside, the little spark

Bobby is always talking about is igniting into something bigger. I feel like Drew Barrymore in the movie *Firestarter*.

God help this man. If I get the slightest opportunity, I may kill him.

"Good, let the pain be a reminder to behave. You can earn your freedom by purging your soul. Let's start with your transgressions. I'll say them, and you'll ask for forgiveness. Are you ready?"

Transgressions? What the hell is he talking about? Not wanting to earn his wrath, I obediently say, "Yes, sir."

"You fixed me up with Tommy. I'm not gay, you little bitch." He glares at me, waiting.

"I'm sorry. You'd been spending a lot of time in the bar, a gay bar. I misinterpreted. I apologize." I wait for a reaction, but he just nods.

"You didn't listen to your father when he suggested a good match for you. You could've had it made." He hovers over me. His presence is threatening. Add his sinister voice, and it's a combination from hell.

I want to yell out something in my defense, but I'm learning his rules. I'll do what it takes to avoid additional injury. "I'm sorry, my father has always had my best interests at heart." His reaction is unreadable.

"You whore around. You gave yourself to countless men, men who your father did not choose. Admit you're a whore." His voice booms with the last statement. This is personal to him.

I falter. I'm not a whore. I can count my lovers on one hand, and I know fully that few women my age can do that. I try to speak the words, but they get caught in my throat. He pops me in the back of the head.

I spit out the words, "I'm a whore. I'm sorry I disappointed you," I cry.

He drops to his knees in front of me and pulls me to his chest. The stench of cigarettes turns my stomach.

"Shh, it's okay, Rachel. Daddy's here." His lips brush against my hair. "You've been bad, but you'll be better."

I tense. Something has changed. He's no longer the employee intent on pleasing my father. He's the father.

Who's Rachel? What do I say to him?

"I promise to be better."

It's a safe statement. I don't acknowledge his slip. It's scary enough to be kidnapped, but now I realize I have to contend with a man who has lost his connection to reality.

He pushes away from me. "I see what you're trying to do. You're trying to confuse me. You're not

Rachel. Rachel's gone. She wouldn't listen to reason. She..." He walks off without finishing his sentence.

Shit, she's gone? Did he kill her? I can't be sure, but my gut tells me it's true.

"Tell me about your daughter."

"She was just like you. Young, beautiful, and stupid." He mumbles something unintelligible before he walks out the door, locking it behind him.

He left my legs free. I bolt from the chair. This is my moment, my one chance. I listen, but only silence fills the air. Adrenaline once again surges through my veins. I can't feel my injuries. The rush of energy propels me forward. I run to the table, hoping to find something to free my hands. There's nothing but a lighter, some canned goods, and a can opener. My hope plummets. My chest constricts.

Breathe.

Take control of the moment.

Think.

I'm no MacGyver, but there's got to be something I can use. I pace in front of the table. I turn my back to it and pick up a can of peas, along with the can opener. I take three tries to line the blade up with the can. It's difficult with my hands tied behind my back. I clamp down on the handle and turn the crank slowly. I pray I can open the can before he returns. A popping sound fills me with renewed confidence.

With care, I extract the lid and slide the open can into the dark corner, hoping he won't see it.

Thunk, thunk.

His boots hit the wooden porch. My heart drops to my feet. I race to the chair and sit down, tucking the sharp lid under my bottom. A key slides in the lock. He enters and slams the door behind him. In his hands is a bottle of oil and a spatula. He sets the items on the table. My heart stills. I silently pray he doesn't see the open can of peas.

"You were good. You stayed put. That tells me there's hope for you. Rachel wasn't as obedient. She needed a lot of conditioning, and she couldn't be saved."

He walks over to the dark corner and pulls out a folding lounge chair. Its plastic straps are missing in several places. He sets it across the room from me and lies down and closes his eyes. Is he really going to sleep? Now?

Pulling the lid quietly from under my bottom, I grip it, intending to take advantage of this opportunity. Holding on to it the best I can, I saw back and forth working to sever the plastic tie. It cuts through my skin as I hold it in a death grip. The slickness of my blood makes it difficult to grasp, but I work tirelessly.

The seat shifts, and a creak echoes through the silence. He bolts upright.

"What was that sound?" He rises from the chair.

"My seat creaked. I'm sorry to wake you." My voice trembles. I shove the blood-slicked lid under my bottom.

He heaves himself into a standing position and walks around me. I hold my breath, silently begging for him not to find the lid.

"I bet you're wondering when your boyfriend will come to the rescue you. You're a sneaky one. I was wondering why you seemed so calm. My daughter wasn't nearly as calm. Maybe it's because she knew me." He pulls a handful of metal and plastic pieces from his pocket. "I know you, Roxanne. You would never go anywhere without your phone. You lied, and I will punish you."

He tosses the scraps of the phone at my feet. My confidence crashes. I was waiting for Bobby to burst through the door any minute. How will he find me now? It's been hours, and I've been positive and tried to find my way out, but now I can only depend on myself.

He snickers as my shoulders sag.

"I have to go to the bathroom." If he lets my hands free, I can fight with every ounce of strength I have.

"Too bad. I wanted you to behave, and you didn't. You can wait." He steps over to the ratty lounge chair and lies back down. "Don't do anything stupid, Roxanne. I'm not in the mood for your shit tonight. Just sit there and think about your sins. We'll discuss them in the morning."

Stupid man.

I maneuver the lid from under my ass and go back to work on the tie. He must have used an industrial-strength zip tie. The blood on my hand has dried since I hid the lid. Its stickiness has turned into a bonus. The once slippery lid now sits firmly in my glue-like hands. I wince at the pain, but I continue to saw the plastic strip without stopping. Time is crucial.

The hours drag on. He sleeps on the tattered lounge like it's a feather bed. Snores drown out the frantic sawing sound I'm creating behind my back.

Is it morning yet? Throughout the night, my mind replayed all the joyous moments with Bobby.

Tonight was supposed to go differently. I was supposed to dress up and tell Bobby I loved him. Now, I may never get the chance. Theresa was right. If I ever get out of this mess, I'll tell him I love him so many times he'll be sick of hearing it.

Finally, the tie gives in and snaps free. The final crack echoes through the air. He stirs. I hold my breath. Palming the plastic, I stop it from falling to the floor. Blood rushes to my hands; the pain is excruciating, but I push it aside.

"What are you up to over there, my little lotus?"

His voice startles me. Quickly, I shove the lid back under my butt. His feet slide over the edge of the cot, and he stretches and stands. The prickly hairs of his beard rise and fall as his hands rub his face. One step, then another, and he stumbles in his sleepy stupor toward me.

His reference to me being a lotus flower is pissing me off. When the opportunity presents itself, I will rise from the darkness and become pure again. I will rise from the chair and kick his crazy ass.

"Nothing. I shifted again, and the chair squeaked. I've been sitting here for a long time. What time is it?"

"It's time to get started. We have things to do. I've got something special for you. It will hurt, but it will remind you to stay focused." He pulls a small branding iron from his pocket. Shoving it in front of my eyes, the outline of a lotus flower shines under the lantern light.

"Remember, you are a lotus. Today, you will rise from the darkness and be reborn." He walks over to the camp stove and lights it. Will he see the open can? I release my breath when he walks toward me.

He's out of his mind if he thinks I'm going to let him brand me. The iron, warm from his pocket, slides across my cheek before he runs it down the side of my neck. Despite its warmth, the metal chills me to the core. "Where should we put your reminder, Roxanne? Do we want the world to see it, or just you?" Common sense tells me to pull my hands free and fight, but instinct tells me it's not time. The small iron crosses my midriff and continues a path down my leg. Someone once said the eyes are the windows to the soul. Looking into his, I see nothing. A barren waste-land stares back at me. He's empty. Nothing exists beyond the cloudy irises. No soul. No conscience. Nothing. "Maybe we should brand you here." His hand squeezes my private parts.

It's time to act. No one touches me there but Bobby.

I throw my head backward, then forward. His nose collapses against my forehead, and blood runs into my eyes. I'm not sure if it's his blood or mine. I don't care. I pull my hands forward and push him away. He falls to the floor in front of me, clutching his nose. Before he can get up and reach me, I run past him to the table and grab the oil.

"Roxanne, I thought you might be different. Your dad would've been so proud. I would've been so proud." Blood drips from his nose as he staggers to-ward me.

"Don't come any closer. I will set this place on fire, you sick bastard." I pull the lid off the oil bottle. The heat from the stove is singeing my arm hairs. "Give me the keys."

He pulls them from his pocket and waves them

in his bloody hand. "These... you want these?" He tosses them toward the door. "You'll have to come through me to get them, Roxanne. You won't make it." The look on his face is straight out of a horror movie. It's the look Jack Nicholson had just before he axed the door in *The Shining*. Evil—pure evil.

"Bobby, is that his name? You'll never see him again. He's part of your past, Roxanne." Looking around the vacant cabin, he snorts. "This is your future. I'm your future. This is our journey through the darkness and into the light."

The mention of Bobby's name squeezes my heart. I can't think about not seeing him—seeing him is my right. Touching him again will be a reality, and loving him is a given conclusion.

"Don't you dare think of him. He is everything perfect in the world. You—you're nothing. Less than nothing. You're crazy, you stupid loser."

Defiantly, I stare into his eyes. There is no way I'll let him see how terrified I am. My heart pounds as if it will beat its way out of my chest.

Heart skips.

Pulse flutters.

Rapid Breaths.

Pure Terror.

If I'm going to die, I'm going to die fighting.

The smoldering flame, which began as a spark, is now on its way to becoming a full raging inferno. A glance at the oil and then at the fire inspires me. Knowing it's now or never, I squeeze the oil, dousing him from top to toe. Shocked at my action, he lunges forward. I pivot as he falls past me onto the camp stove. I couldn't have choreographed it better.

His screams fill the quiet night. I don't turn around to look. The smell of charred skin burns my nose. I race to find the keys in the dark corner. My sticky fingers connect, and with shaking hands, I unlock the door and run free.

The moon is setting in the distance. The canopy of the trees keeps the road dark. One foot after another, I run down the empty road. My shaking legs take me farther than my body thought capable. It's amazing what a person can do with the proper motivation. Living is motivation number one; finding Bobby is number two.

The lights up ahead nearly blind me. Exhausted, I stop in the center of the road and wave my hands. Flashing lights—I've never been happier to see flashing lights. Falling to my knees in the center of the road, I weep.

When I feel powerful arms surround me, I bury my face in my rescuer's chest. His scent replaces the smell of burning flesh. *Thank God.* Pine with citrus envelope me. It's the scent of everything right in my life. It's the scent of love. It's Bobby.

He transfers me to the waiting ambulance but

refuses to leave my side and climbs aboard. It takes a moment for me to realize the commotion surrounding me is my wretched cries. I try to speak, but Bobby tells me to breathe and that he has me. I inhale and wail again.

It's over. It's finally over.

CHAPTER TWENTY-FOUR

My eyes strain to focus on my surroundings.
Something heavy is on my legs. Bobby is sprawled
across me, and his arms cage my body
protectively. *My protector.* I raise my bandaged palms
to his hair—his beautiful hair. The movement stirs
him, and he lifts his eyes to mine. Dark circles sit beneath his emerald-green orbs. Oh, he's a sight to see—
an incredible vision. Emotions threaten to choke me
again.

I was crying, then nothing. They must have given
me something to put me out.

"Hey, how are you? Are you in pain?" He rubs
his hand up my leg.

I feel like I dropped from an airplane without
a parachute. There isn't a piece of me that

doesn't hurt, but I feel fabulous. Pain means I made it.

"Oh, Bobby." Tears rush from my eyes.

His eyes pop open, and he attempts to stand. "I'll get the nurse."

I grab for his hand, pulling him back. "I love you. I've always loved you, and I'll always love you. I'm so sorry I didn't tell you before now."

He folds his body into the tiny space beside me. Gently, he brings my hand to his lips. "I know, Roxy. I'll love you forever, too." We stay in the moment until the nurse informs Bobby visiting hours are over.

He asks the nurse for a few more minutes, and thankfully she grants his request.

I follow his gaze to the object sitting on top of the table. His phone sits silently next to me.

"How did you find me? I hid my phone, but he found it and destroyed it. I thought I'd never see you again."

"I'm so proud of you. You kept your head through the entire ordeal. I only found you because you thought to hide your phone. We followed the signal into the mountains, and then we lost you. I thought about the lotus and the message on your wall. The sayings were too close to be a simple coincidence."

"It was Mason. I mean, Jason."

"Yes, he changed the first letter of his name to stay under the radar. I called in some favors and found out Jason Mack owned some land in the mountains. That's how we got to you. I'm only sorry I didn't get to you sooner. I tried."

"Oh, Fletch. You came. *You* saved me. I was so afraid of having to give you up, but I refused to let that happen."

His shaky lips touch mine. His whole body quakes. "You won't ever have to give me up."

I pull him tight against me. With his face buried in my hair, I hold him while he cries. I'll never embarrass him by reminding him of the tears. Compared to my heartless father, who would never shed a tear for a family member, Bobby's obvious love and adoration is something I'll always treasure. I'm loved. I'm safe. I'm home.

My injuries are minor, but the doctor is concerned about the psychological trauma and demands I stay for several days.

My room smells more like a florist than a hospital. Mixed bouquets and Gerbera daisies of every color cover every surface. Bobby doesn't show up without them. He leaves me only when the night nurse kicks him out.

Kat, Emma, Anthony, Damon, Chris, and Trevor have all been to visit. Chris painted my toenails and said no girl should be seen without a proper pedicure.

Theresa came to visit. Her eyes filled with tears as she looked me over. It took a nurse and Bobby to pry her away. The woman hugged and rocked me for hours. I don't understand how a woman who barely knows me could love me so openly and with such irresistible warmth. I remember asking how a single woman could raise three small boys on her own after losing the love of her life. I now know. It's simple. Like her son, she loves profusely, unconditionally, and with grand passion.

Even my parents came for a visit. My father looked pained when he saw my black and blue face and my bandaged hands. He didn't apologize. That's not his style. The fact he showed up says a lot. My mother lost her composure the minute she saw me, and the staff had to sedate her and get her a room.

I met my nieces for the first time. It was awkward when my sisters showed up. It had been so many years, but after a brief lull in the conversation, we were able to catch up in just under two hours. Roseanne's little girls make excellent icebreakers.

It took two days, but Bobby finally asked me about the night. He didn't want me to relive it, but he needed to know. I agreed to tell the story once and made him promise never to ask again. In no way did I want the ordeal to influence our future.

He brought in a police officer to record my statement, and I'll forever be grateful I took the time to think things through. Bobby's voice in my head telling me to think made the difference between life and death, and his praise for my courage increased as I recited the nightmare to my best recollection.

I was his captive for over five hours. At times, it seemed like five minutes, at others, five years.

Bobby filled in the blanks. He'd raced to pick me up from the bar, but when he arrived, all he found was a box of letters spilled on the sidewalk. No one had seen me since I ran out thirty minutes before. He took an hour to get to the police station, file the report, and track my phone.

His body shakes as he relives the night.

At the conclusion, I look up to find his face ashen —tormented. It's my turn to comfort him. I reach for his hands and ask one more question. I'm not sure I want the truth, but I need the truth.

"Is he dead?"

How will I feel if I took his life? I didn't set him on fire, although I would have if it came down to it. I doused him with oil, and if he's dead, I'll feel responsible.

"No, he survived, but he can't hurt you. He'll go to jail for the rest of his life. We found the remains of his daughter buried behind the cabin."

The impact of that statement rocks my foundation. He killed his child, so he would've killed me.

"You saved me, Bobby. You were there every minute, talking to me, telling me the things I needed to do. Without you, I wouldn't be here."

"I wish I'd been there." His eyes fill with tears of despair.

"You were there, and you were here." My hand covers my heart.

THE DAY I'M RELEASED, Bobby arrives with new clothes. He gently brushes my hair and helps me apply my makeup. Who knew he had those skills? We walk to the car hand in hand. As he kisses me with incredible tenderness, my heart nearly explodes.

"We have to take a detour on our way to my apartment. I hope it's okay."

I smile at him. "Where you're going, I'm going. By the way, have I told you I love you today?"

"Yes, you have, but I'll listen to you say those words repeatedly and never tire of the sound." He buckles me into my seat like a child and walks to his side of the car.

"You understand I'm not a fragile being, right?" He's been treating me with caution since the kidnapping.

"I know you're not. You're a total badass. I'm not cautious because I'm worried for you. I'm cautious because I'm worried for myself. You might go all MacGyver on me." He winks at me, and we both erupt into laughter. Everything will be fine.

Being out of the hospital feels terrific, and I'll never take the freedom to move around for granted again. He pulls in front of Emma's house, and I look at him with curiosity.

Is this part of my healing process?

"Is it too soon? I don't want you to go in if you don't feel comfortable." His eyes look between the house and me.

"No, it's fine. I have only good memories here. I love this house." I don't wait for him to open the car door. I throw it open and walk up the sidewalk. "Is it ready?" Will I want to move back in? I love the house, but I love Bobby more.

He doesn't say a word. He walks to the door with a smile on his face. He pulls a key from his pocket, and I look at him with a thousand questions in my mind, the first one being, *How did he get a key to the house?*

The lock clicks as he turns the key, and the door swings open to a fully refurbished house. My foot lifts to step inside, but he stops me mid-stride.

He pulls an envelope from his coat pocket and

holds it in front of me. My head tilts, and my mind races. What's this beautiful man up to?

"Roxy Somerville, I bought this house for you. I made the deal last week after you mentioned Anthony wanted Emma to sell it." He hands me the purchase agreement. I was right; he had been up to something. "I want you to live here with me, but not as a Somerville. I want you to be an Anderson." He drops to one knee and pulls a little black box from his pants pocket. He flips it open and presents me with a beautiful diamond ring. "Roxy, it may be too soon for you, but I'm willing to wait forever if I have to. My future doesn't exist without you." His hands shake. "I lost you once, and it won't happen again. Everything about us is so easy, so perfect. You belong with me. Be mine forever?" I look into his eyes and see my future.

Happy tears stream down my face. I'm rarely speechless, but he caught me completely off guard. There are so many unnamable emotions going through me that I feel faint. *He bought me the house. Do I want to marry him? Yes, a thousand times, yes.* All I can do is nod, but that is enough, it seems.

A smile as big as Texas takes over his face. He slips the traditionally set, timeless ring on my finger. The simple solitaire sits in the center of a platinum band. *Beautiful.*

Finally, I find my voice. "How did you do all of this?"

He rises to his feet.

"First things first, I want to kiss my future bride. Then I'm going to carry you over the threshold and into our new house." He's a man of his word. He kisses me senseless, and just when my knees buckle, he picks me up and carries me into the house—our house.

I walk with him through each room. Everything is new. It's the perfect place to begin again. I notice a few additions, like the state-of-the-art security system installed. No one will ever get near this house again without being seen. He walks me to the master bedroom, and a king-sized bed sits dead center. On top of the comforter is a football, and written across the pigskin is, "Fletch loves Firefly."

We spend the rest of the afternoon making love in our new house. Replete, I lie across his chest, admiring my ring. I've worn nothing as beautiful as his promise.

"It is my mother's ring. She wants you to have it. She says her marriage was filled with love and passion, and she wants the same for us." He holds my hand and looks at the ring he put on my finger. "She fell in love with you the minute she saw you. You have that effect on the Andersons."

"You Andersons are easy to love." We lie in bed

until our stomachs demand attention, and when I can no longer ignore the grumbling, we crawl out of bed and dress. At the front door, we find a letter.

Bobby bends down to retrieve the envelope. It's addressed to Roxanne Somerville from the Law Offices of Clark and Stratton. I palm the letter and walk with Bobby out the door.

"I just forwarded our mail. Emma had yours forwarded to my apartment the day you moved in. I wasn't sure how long the renovations would take. You don't get much mail."

On a mission to find food, I wait until I'm in the car to open the letter. We decide to go back to the restaurant where we had our first date. Once I am buckled in, I slide my finger under the flap and tear the envelope open, and I read the top page and laugh.

"What's so funny?" He glances at me and then focuses his eyes back on the road.

"You bought me a house and made me an offer I couldn't refuse. I'm going to do something for you today as well."

"What could you give me that I don't already have?"

"How about millions of dollars?"

He pulls over and slams on the brakes. The envelope falls from my hands. "What do you mean?"

"My trust fund has caught up with me. My grandparents were very generous." I pick up the letter from the floor and place it on his lap. He stares at the seven, followed by six zeros. "I guess we can afford to furnish our house."

His mouth drops open. I made him speechless.

"This is your money." He folds the letter and puts it on my lap.

"No, we're together, and everything belongs to us. The funny thing is, I've been living paycheck to paycheck for four years, and all this time, I've been a millionaire. What's even funnier is, I haven't missed being rich. Do you think it will change us?"

He pauses for a moment before he replies. "Yes," he says, "we'll have softer sheets."

I tell the man we have over seven million dollars, and all he wants are softer sheets. God, I love him.

EPILOGUE

Six Months Later

"Is everyone here?" Emma's round belly enters the room first. Anthony hovers over his wife like a bodyguard. Their first child will be born in four months. Pregnancy agrees with her, judging by her glowing complexion.

"Yes." Kat approaches the front of the room, looking breathtaking in a beautiful white lace wedding gown. Standing behind her is Chris. He looks great in his white tuxedo. The sequined bowtie is a bit over the top, but Chris likes bling. Last in line is me. I opted for something simple. A white silk shift glides over my body. I'm more interested in my wedding night than my wedding dress.

Emma, the drill sergeant, gets us lined up just as

the music plays. It's odd for Pachelbel's "Canon in D" to play while we march toward Elvis. All three brides have their sights set on one person. For Kat, it's Damon, for Chris, it's Trevor, and for me, it's Bobby. It's always been Bobby, and it always will be.

All three of us line up in front of Elvis. Every seat in the chapel is full. Two brides and four grooms can fill a venue.

Elvis starts the ceremony by performing "It's Now or Never" and ends with "Love Me Tender." When he says you may kiss your bride, no one needs prodding. It's Elvis, and he's the King.

Marrying in Vegas was Damon's idea, but all three grooms were on board the minute he suggested a triple wedding. For the three couples, the wedding wasn't important. It was the commitment that meant everything. Sharing the event with our best friends was priceless.

We leave the Chapel of Love and go straight to the reception. Anthony Haywood's of Las Vegas is hosting the celebration. Emma tried to talk the group into tattoos before, but there were no takers.

"Roxy, you are a beautiful bride." Theresa hugs me, and she whispers in my ear, then she walks away with a smile on her face.

"What was that about?"

Bobby pulls me into his arms, and it's the perfect place for me. It's the place I feel loved, cherished, and safe. I look around the room and catch the envious stares of my sisters. They chose differently. They valued things that didn't appeal to me. They wanted big houses, nice cars, and fancy clothes. I wanted a soul mate, someone who'd share my life, not run it. Everything I want and need begins and ends with Bobby.

"Your mother informed me she would like a grandchild within the year. I suggest we say goodbye to our guests so we can go to our room and practice."

"My mother is awesome." He picks me up and tosses me over his shoulder. "Say goodbye, Firefly. My mom has never asked for anything. I'd like to grant her this wish. Are you game?"

"We're in this together, Fletch. Lead on."

We slip out of the reception. The only one who appears to notice is Theresa, who jumps up and down like a woman who just won the lottery.

AFTER A SHORT HONEYMOON IN HAWAII, we returned to our new life in our new home. I'd quit my job at the bar and persuaded Anthony to start an Anthony Haywood Academy for teens. I donated the start-up money to help disadvantaged youth learn about the culinary arts. Anthony and Damon matched me dollar for dollar.

I never expected my return on investment to be so fruitful. Young people need options. Everyone is pushing them in different directions, and we need to be reminded we have choices. There is no greater joy than to help someone take control of a moment. Each moment can stretch into a lifetime.

I even got my dad involved. He's not a great father, but he's an excellent lawyer, and he took no time at all to draw up the legal documents for the culinary academy.

Emma gave birth to a baby girl three months and twenty-two days after the mass wedding. Chloe was eager to enter the world. She arrived with a full head of red hair and a scream that could be heard worldwide.

By the time she made her appearance, Kat was just getting over her morning sickness. Damon looked stunned when Kat broke the news at a group dinner. She didn't tell him in advance because she wanted the group to witness his reaction. The man wept with joy.

Chris and Trevor are as solid as ever. They have traded in their Friday nights at Trax to become the official babysitters for Emma and Anthony. Kat and Damon have secured their future Saturdays.

Bobby and I haven't granted Theresa's wish, but we aren't quitters; we practice every chance we get. We understand life sometimes has its own pace, and if we are honest, we are thankful to have that time to be with each other. Losing those years where we could've been together was hard, but it has also enabled us never to take for granted our second chance at love. Sometimes, the best things in life can't be rushed.

OTHER BOOKS BY KELLY COLLINS

A Pure Decadence Series

Yours to Have

Yours to Conquer

Yours to Protect

A Pure Decadence Collection

Recipes for Love

A Tablespoon of Temptation

A Pinch of Passion

A Dash of Desire

A Cup of Compassion

A Dollop of Delight

A Layer of Love

Recipe for Love Collection 1-3

Recipe for Love Collection 4-6

ABOUT THE AUTHOR

International bestselling author of more than thirty novels, Kelly Collins writes with the intention of keeping love alive. Always a romantic, she blends real-life events with her vivid imagination to create characters and stories that lovers of contemporary romance, new adult, and romantic suspense will return to again and again.

For More Information
www.authorkellycollins.com
kelly@authorkellycollins.com

Printed in Great Britain
by Amazon

34810163R00155

– Pour Esteban,
le rayon de soleil de ses parents.
M.

– Pour Anaïs.
L. R.

Bali

Papa

Maman

© Flammarion, 2011
Éditions Flammarion – 87, quai Panhard-et-Levassor – 75647 Paris Cedex 13
www.editions.flammarion.com
ISBN : 978-2-0812-4983-7 – N° d'édition : L.01EJDN000657.C004
Dépôt légal : août 2011
Imprimé en Espagne par Edelvives – 01/2013
Loi n° 49-956 du 16 juillet 1949 sur les publications destinées à la jeunesse
TM Bali est une marque déposée de Flammarion

Magdalena

Bali™
va à l'école

Laurent Richard

Père Castor ▪ Flammarion

Aujourd'hui, c'est la rentrée.
Bali va à l'école pour la première fois.

Bali a mis des chaussures neuves,
mais elles lui font un peu mal aux pieds.
Maman lui donne son cartable.
– Comme tu es grand, maintenant, mon Bali.

Sur le chemin de l'école, Bali répète :
– Je suis grand, maintenant,
je vais à l'école comme un grand.

Mais tout à coup, Bali demande :
— Maman, tu n'oublieras pas de venir me chercher ?
— Voyons, mon Bali, une maman n'oublie jamais
son grand fils chéri.

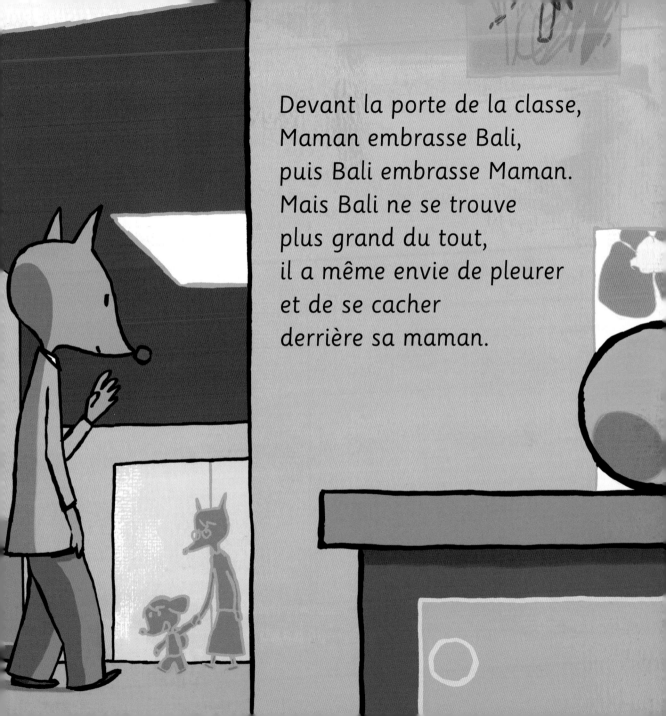

Devant la porte de la classe,
Maman embrasse Bali,
puis Bali embrasse Maman.
Mais Bali ne se trouve
plus grand du tout,
il a même envie de pleurer
et de se cacher
derrière sa maman.

– Bonjour, je m'appelle Sabine,
dit la maîtresse en caressant la tête de Bali.
– Bonjour, je suis la maman de Bali.
– Bonjour, marmonne timidement Bali.

– Voici ta classe, dit la maîtresse.
Tu peux aller jouer avec tes nouveaux amis.

Bali lâche la main de Maman
et s'avance tout doucement.

Soudain, Bali sent quelqu'un lui tapoter l'épaule.
– Coucou Bali, c'est moi ! Je t'attendais, dit Tamara.
Mais on dirait que tu as envie de pleurer,
tu n'es pas content d'aller à l'école ?

Bali répond en mentant un peu :
– C'est à cause de mes chaussures neuves,
elles me font mal aux pieds.
– Viens mettre tes chaussons, dit Tamara.
L'école c'est un peu comme à la maison.

– J'y vais, Bali. Passe une bonne journée,
dit Maman rassurée.

– Au revoir, Maman ! répond Bali sans lever le nez.

– Il est déjà très occupé, dit la maîtresse Sabine
en riant.